Parable Terminus

The Parable Collection, Volume 6

Christopher Besonen

Published by Besonen Horror, 2023.

Copyright

This is a work of fiction. Names, places, characters, businesses, places, events or incidents are written in a fictitious manner, or an output of the author's imagination. Any resemblance to any actual persons, living or dead, or actual events, is purely coincidental.

All text contained within this book, rather digital or physical, is protected by copyright law. ©2021-2023. All rights reserved unto Christopher Daniel Besonen, the author, courtesy of the Besonen Horror trademark. No unlicensed reproductions of this book may be used, without written consent by Mr. Besonen.

Dedication:

In memoriam of no one.

War Against The Seen

"He removed his remaining eye. They are treating him now."

The Leader didn't have to ask who, the infamous killer had taken out his other eye previously, blaming them as having offended him. Sourcing Biblical reasons for the maiming.

"We can handle him, later. We have a situation," The Leader replied, shifting his focus to The Scanner.

"It never ends, does it?"

The inquiry was from the newest member to join the cause.

"It is why you're here. Why we do what we do," The Leader said, never once pulling his attention from The Scanner.

They had no name, a few had titles, but they were mainly just people determined to carry out justice, and implement prevention.

"You still think about her, don't you?"

"The case affected me, that woman didn't deserve what happened to her. That coward blamed his past, others blame demons. Not us, we blame the individual. Free will makes each of us culpable."

The newbie nodded to agree, then prepared for the first mission. To prove loyalty, this member was to kill the aforementioned blind party.

It needed to be done.

It was the one named by the new member as the case that solidified the decision to join up. Hearts torn from a mother and her children, it was too much. The man who had gouged his eyes out needed to see true reform.

The Leader had only recently decided that it was time to act. Internet forums had brought The Group together. Sickened by the evil that people do, they each picked a crime that disturbed them the most, then executed the culprit. The Leader had paved the way when he took out a major coward who had thrown boiling water on his once joyful wife. A kind soul who found a monster, one that used affection as manipulation to control her. Abuse was rampant, physically and mentally. She stayed, eventually it became a decision that would end her life. She would be tortured for days after the boiling water incident, her body was found with multiple broken bones, terrible bruising and air gun pellet holes. A beautiful life ended in agony. It was nothing new, the system was broken, all of them. The Leader knew this, so the cowardly husband was paid a visit. Ensuring the correct guards were on duty, the guilty was left alone in a section of the prison far from the others. An isolated cell, where The Leader was waiting with The Group. The prisoner was grabbed and immediately his tongue was nailed to the wall. Using rusty, but sharpened, surgical tools, the prisoners' guts were pulled out and lacerated in sections. Piece by piece, the contents spilled out in foul secretions as The Group, along with their Leader, attached various pieces around the cell. Later reports would state that the intestines were coming out of the stomach, mouth, eyes and anus, all while keeping the murdering wife abuser living through each painful moment. Further analysis of the corpse would notate that every single nerve in the limbs were pulled out so that their endings were sitting just beyond the surface of the dermis. The prisoner lived for a short period, enduring only a fraction of what he had done to the one he claimed he loved, the one he had vowed to.

The Group did the same to the eyeless prisoner, this time overseen by the latest recruit, who excitedly made macabre art. When they were finished, The Leader made a simple statement before they left the scene and their patient.

"He's cured."

There was a sense of accomplishment amongst The Group and their Leader.

"The Bible would tell us that a Judgment Day awaits. Meanwhile, our justice systems fail us time and time again. Why wait? The great day of vengeance can be daily, that is our purpose. Some will call us vigilantes, but others will refer to us as heroes, crusaders. My dream is to inspire forced change. Forgiveness and grace, they're almost beyond human comprehension. For we are all allotted free will, therefore each individual is responsible for their own deeds. May God forgive our undertaking, but our mission will continue with, or without, His permission. A life sentence is granted, tell me, how does anything even out when a perpetrator that only dealt death is gifted life? There is only one word that can solve the problem, balance."

The Group felt prideful as their Leader spoke, this was the crusade they were born for.

"We are warriors against injustice."

"Hi, sorry to bother you, I was wondering if I can get a ride a block over to get some gas. Mine ran out, silly me. This has never happened before and I feel idiotic."

"Sure, get in," the driver behind the wheel of the running car replied.

When she was in, The Creep immediately changed his demeanor and got aggressive. His hand went to her left thigh without permission, he kept looking in the back seat, prompting an uneasiness in the passenger.

"What do you keep looking at?"

"My four year old daughter, she has a gun pointed at your skull and is well trained in how to shoot, experienced too," the man replied with an eerie calmness.

He smiled, forced the stranger in his vehicle to kiss him, then pressured her to show herself to him. She was feeling nauseous and uncomfortable, even as she complied with everything he demanded from her. This wasn't the man's first assault and it would be far from his last. The incident would be attached to the expanding list in a string of similar situations and attacks.

"We have agencies that swear to protect and do not, pulpits where preying wolves deliver messages of hope and security, so many that claim they want to live in a better place but prove otherwise in their actions. They state that they want to make a difference, to be the difference. They're liars, deceitful. Hundreds anticipate Heaven, never once stopping to realize that our Earth can represent paradise. We can mirror it, the outcome of our cause will be a reflection of our Utopia. Cleansed of the wicked, the good living in harmony rather than bound by fear, pain and anxiety. Dozens of people take ownership of being alive, never realizing that the trepidation stemming from a society and world gone mad makes their existence less than death itself. There is a solution, the answer to solve the problem lies within eradication. The shortest distance between two points is a straight line. We are the pivotal points for the equation.

For years, I spent life on the front lines fighting crime. All I ever saw were reminders of what had to be done. I tried to do it their way, how the others before me paved paths of reform, I went and I tried to conform and do these things legally. It was only after repeated failures, that I found my true calling. A once bubbly woman full of dreams was scalded and tortured to death, the case permanently switched on what I had always repressed. My turning point, just as each of you heard your own cases that made you want to cry out for a revolution. Too many lives are cut short, meanwhile the ones responsible breath inside a cell as if they deserve to be alive. Simply put, there is no room for patience when it comes to extinguishing evil. Turning the other cheek, grace for all, these are not plausible ideas on an irrational Earth. They are words lovely on a page, but reality beckons something else to be done. The dead scream for reckoning, and it has come."

The Group uttered phrases of agreement, each of their brains swirling with the shared desire to snuff out more flames of decadence.

"The weak see Hell as a place to be fearful of, but the strong know it is a land of rectification. Admirable, Hell is a reflection of The Almighty's wrath. Such a spot must exist, just as what it is we are doing must. Our duty is to purify our realm."

They all then turned their attentions to The Scanner, there was a house nearby with a child in danger. Following the directions provided through The Scanner, they came up to an expensive house. An ideal home for most, but a habitat for nightmares to the oldest daughter. Her mother had passed away, leaving her in the care of a voyeur and pervert. A man who liked to have the 'party house', enjoyed having the girl's friends over, all the while he was secretly recording and abusing them once they were intoxicated.

The Scanner was The Group's most valuable asset. An individual from another dimension, one with incredible abilities. Not only were there elements of being psychic with The Scanner, but also a quality of time travelling abilities. The waves scanned were interdimensional, The Group never knew when or where they would end up, but the crime details were always precise. If there was punishment due, it would be located in the scanning.

"All things have consequence, everything leaves an imprint that echoes in all planes. The choices made by us all, effect us all. It is why we scan for traumatic hotspots. Any area with residue from a traumatic event can erupt any number of atrocities in the future. We are the tongues of the deceased, the voice of reason in an unreasonable reality. Laws protect the wrong ones, therefore they must be ignored. Same with Biblical passages. We believe in Holy text, yes, but we stand firmly against the call for peace. This is our destiny, our actions are battles against flesh and blood. We honor every victim when we implement amends. Now, let us do our ritual and prevent another statistic."

All but The Scanner exited the unmarked van, they went into the two story house, then they erased the abuser. Hands tainted in stolen innocence were held up to seek mercy, but only found the pleas ignored. Just as he refused to stop night after night, incident after incident. The Group was revealing hidden things, these deletions were scriptural according to their hearts and thought processes. They were happy with a full Hell if it equated purification.

"I can stop," were the only words uttered by the predator, spoken through quivering lips.

"We know you can," was the only reply allotted to the former Cop.

"Look into the eyes of survivors of trauma based happenings, the soul's gateway cannot conceal their brokenness. A lifetime of recovery is what is left ahead for the victims, while those responsible reminisce their actions, often with pleasure. The notion is unbalanced. This, of course, only has effects on those still living, countless families aren't granted such a luxury, their loved ones are no longer with us. Layers of pain, this is what the selfish leave behind for their legacy. Legal systems are not enacted to bring order, but control and profit. The only protection against fresh offenses is to eliminate the threats. There's no rehabilitation, that has been shown as factual again and again, so we offer up the one true remedy to incurable sicknesses."

The lady in the passenger seat sobbed, she had survived so much in life, only to end up in another trap. She wasn't alone, there were many instances of this type of cycle, almost as if doors were left open by past inflections. Entryways for further damage. Invisible connections that worked together for the purpose of evil. The digital age only worsened things, it was easier than ever to distribute evidence among the hordes that crave deviance. Such proof only spawned more circles for the disease to spread to.

The thought of a toddler pointing a gun at her was unbearable and her crying intensified.

"Are you going to kill me?"

The inquiry made the driver chuckle. He gently squeezed her thigh, his eyes glazing over with a malicious gleam.

"Never. I want to be in your memories forever, and ever."

He then pounced upon his latest trophy, as she wept for the child in the backseat, the circumstance reminded her of what she had endured growing up. Though they weren't similar in specifics, they still shared a common ground.

When the man was done using her, he forced her to kiss him and admit affections that she didn't mean. Once he felt content in her humiliation, he slapped her and forced her out of the car naked. He then drove off in satisfaction, while his sufferer bawled and dressed herself in the empty parking lot.

"Forgiveness is to enable. Absolving personal accountability only reinforces to the deranged that their ways were acceptable. Justification cannot be allowed, just as their survival cannot."

The Group listened intently to their Leader as he articulated his views, their collective conclusions expressed through his wise words. No matter where, or when, they went, any evidence meant to bring light to a case was often stored away and forgotten. The media and public officials kept the truth hushed behind motives. They were about to learn precisely why this was, as their van idled outside of another broken home.

The social worker gathered up every disturbing detail, taking notes and offering reassurances that she was there to help. Her rapport with the young boy made him spill everything, he entrusted her to save him. Devastation was all he felt as he was left in the house with his mom, and the nice lady who had promised to provide assistance drove away without him. He noticed that his sign that had prompted concerned neighbors to call social services initially was also taken from his window. His picture, personal information, and home address was then sent out to a private server. On the other end, crooked officials all the way up the chain made plans to ensure the kid would be on a missing person poster. The Scanner passed all of this disheartening information to The Group. Unaware, the info was also presented to a nearby neighbor accidentally, which would recruit the listener after she heard that children taken from homes were being strategically placed with those that would undoubtedly keep up the abuse in their own ways. Those with access to multiple little ones, or that had video proof of their deeds, were given bonuses. The same ones doing all off the trafficking and distribution of illegal material were the very ones that were catching lower level perps and acting as if they had made an improvement in the world.

Each target was tracked, not all abductions were random. A fraction of it was all orchestrated from the top, offering street scum lesser sentences and such in exchange for the kidnappings. The more eavesdropping that was done, the more the listener felt compelled to do something, anything. There was a web of people involved in this, from school counselors to preachers to politicians, and everyone in between. The corruption, greed and perversion seemingly had no limitations.

"It goes as high as you can imagine. They'd bribe God if they were able to," The Scanner said in closure, a tear in the eye.

The intestinal tract display, nerve exposure murders went on for a year after the neighbor had overheard the information uncovered by The Scanner. Everything was kept quiet on the media front about the growing murder case, another limb of corruption. The entire time The Group was disemboweling creeps, the neighbor was silently rallying up her own movement. After a toddler was brutalized with a pipe wrench, the neighbor decided it was the proper moment she had been seeking to act. She went to the prison where the culprit was being held, found his cell, wired his body with implanted explosives and gifted him the death penalty with little bursts. When the bombing hit the news, it was a signal to the others that had agreed to her cause, who then detonated their own instant sentences to prisoners across the state.

She utilized her own abilities and tracked the serial assaulter. The victims had hit over a thousand now and the numbers were increasing. She knew The Group would be unable to locate him because the perp was also a Scanner. Two Scanners could not read one another, but she could. She was a Finder, a bounty hunter that was meant to assassinate both Scanners.

The Creep looped the parking lot areas with frustration, he had been hunting for hours to find someone with the correct shoes on, but still his luck was depleted.

It had been eight long years since his four year old was murdered for a pair of sneakers. They were plain, inexpensive, yet still she was robbed of everything over them. It was cruel to be granted life without an option. If he were shown what would have been, he would have denied his birth. For a brief second, the man contemplated what his daughter would think of his heinous behavior that he was doing in response to her tragedy. Before empathy could take a hold, he spotted a woman wearing the color of shoes that all of his victims wore. He pulled up beside her car, then did his routine.

"Hi. So sorry to be a bother, but my toddler is missing, haven't seen a little one loose, have you?"

The Creep was handsome and friendly, he pulled off the worried dad prose exceptionally well. She got in his vehicle under the premise of providing him assistance, then he took her to the farthest lot and let out his true self. He ravaged the unsuspecting woman, his impulses feeding off of his irritation of the extended hunt. His scanning ability didn't have a setting for specific footwear, so he could only use his natural skills to help him select his prey. Once he was done with the violation, he grabbed her by the hair and smashed her cranium through the passenger window. He then sawed her neck across the splintered shards until she was nearly decapitated. Like he always did, The Creep kept her shoes as a souvenir. He cursed himself for accidentally spilling her blood on them, it then hit him what he had done. He escalated to murder. He felt an even better release from the homicide than he did the mental wounds he normally inflicted. He felt himself ready for the upgrade, he would now be silencing his catches.

The Group was in their secret lair.

"So, when you take an inadequate system that runs on indifference, lazy and corrupt official employees, laws that protect the perpetrators over the victims, bribery, and mass quantities of media that push society to be sexual and is rewiring moral structure, not to mention loops of radio loops played that promote promiscuity and covetousness, I ask of you my family, what do you get?"

"You get a huge problem that needs addressed, immediately," The Finder interrupted, startling The Group.

"How'd you find us?"

"The Scanner," she answered, nodding in The Scanner's direction.

"Explain now... please," The Leader demanded.

"My people exist to find and kill Scanners, there haven't been many and they are masters at hiding. There are people within your realm who are thinning the veils, opening portals, etc. I am from a parallel Earth, things are opposite there and while Scanners pick up on thought patterns, I can hear the impulsive thoughts of the mind. A Scanner's is typically pure, but there's another one with a heart as black as an abyss. He's making a lot of negative buzz in the press, I am sure you're aware of what I'm referencing. Your Scanner cannot find him, it is an impossibility. I was tracking him when I found your Group. I can hear him when he hunts, I'll lead you to him, but there's something you must do for me."

"A thousand voices tell me to hear you. What do you have in mind?"

The woman presented a map of a nearby city with red marks all over it.

"There is an example of how many registered offenders live in a single city.

Here is the county."

The amount of marks of red made each member of The Group boil inside with hatred.

"The state..."

The woman then folded back an overlay that had blue marks.

"These are ones I know about that are still under investigation, or still unknown about. I am sure your Scanner can provide more details."

A wave of nausea took over The Group, when she was done, their entire state was purple.

"Worldwide, it remains purple. Since I first encountered your Group, I have been traveling. I've built quite a following myself and I told them about your Group. They are willing to follow your examples. The Creep's display will be their signal to move into position. The shoes that are in the trunk are the links between the victims, the Police haven't released that detail yet."

Once she had laid out her plan, The Leader formed a verbal pact with her. The verdict was in, a new level of retribution would soon be unleashed.

The Finder led The Group to a parking lot, late at night. The car of The Creep was there, he was asleep inside with a dead woman by his side.

A man with electricity in his eyes was walking up to the car, a briefcase was in his hand. The Group pulled out of the lot just as the briefcase was being opened, whoever the stranger was, The Finder told them that the affair did not concern them and it would be handled. She trembled at the thoughts coming from the man.

First to respond on the scene would describe what they saw as a fountain of electric bursting from the man's midsection. There were a thousand shoe strings dangling from the bolts. He was found displayed on top of piles of the same color of footwear.

The Scanner no longer received readings about the parking lot assaults after, no body else would die, or be taken against their will, at the hands of the culprit.

The Scanner mediated for hours, writing the names of potential allies down. The Finder was telling of a few propositions she had been offered to utilize her nature by the very ones that The Group were on to way to see.

"Why do they want The Scanners assassinated?"

"Cover up, what else? Scanners equal exploitation. There are a lot in power that love to taint innocence, they do it because it is as close as they can damage a part of God. Some act in ritual, others just cannot control their impulsive perversions."

The Leader sat quietly, as did The Group. The Scanner stayed focused, contacting the allies and lining up directly with their patterns of thought. Once each were aligned with the transmission, The Scanner's fingers traced over the map pages, one by one. Drawing the pictures upon their imaginations.

"Guess we will know if they accept soon enough," The Leader noted aloud as the mental fax went out.

"You didn't disclose everything," The Scanner confronted with an inquisitive intrigue.

"I have my own personal mission."

"Back spaces?"

"Yes. Aside from impulse monitoring, I also am ingrained with a technology that uses algorithms to alert me to concerning deletions. Things people start to type, but decide it best not to leave a trail. Writers that put in things as confessional fantasies, then take them out. There are many confessions in the back spaces. I know whom, and what their deleted words say, then I handle it as I deem fit."

"Very fascinating."

"Your Leader has always sought reform, it shall be done. I'm just a required vessel."

The Group was making gutsy décor in a prison block when they heard the news report about an entire neighborhood that had just exploded. They kept on with their ritual, as more bulletins were breaking about other attacks on residential areas. Twelve hours later, more would detonate, this was a cleansing and liberation. This was what becomes a necessity when you have an incompetent government with tainted agencies that miscarry authority and subsequently failed their citizens.

The Group traveled to their next destination, as their Followers lit more fuses and more blasts were timed for future ignition. They would start with the offenders, then move on to those who chose greed and apathy over justice. There could be no room for empathy, innocence was almost as existent as the flesh war's extension of mercy.

"I saw the words you deleted. You are a parasite and it is my place to eliminate scum like you," The Finder scolded, repeating the expunctions back to her latest victim before lining his insides with strands of microscopic explosive devices that would completely rupture everything internally while leaving no marks on the outside.

The Finder stayed until the initial bomb went off, then went forth with the rest of the itinerary.

Adventures In Dread

Chapter 1:

The Parallel Location

Graham followed the coordinates in the letter, anticipation gripped firmly around his mind. It wasn't addressed to him, nor was it marked whom it had came from. Even so, Graham knew when he read it that it was an ailment of fate

The special glasses that came along with the map allowed Graham to see remnants of past traumatic events. Graham looked up at the hills of the roller coasters and grinned, his heart skipping a few beats. In another time, it had been the place of a massacre at the hands of twins. The vision of what they had done was the perfect entanglement of chaos. He imagined that it must mirror how God sees the various intersecting timelines and paths of His creation, deciding where the accidents would be fatal, and who would be spared and when.

"All things reflect," he smiled with a sparkle in his eye.

Graham then removed his glasses and began construction.

Chapter 2:
Opening Day

The opening day was by invite only. A few families without any ties to Graham were given invitations with cash attachments to help coerce their participation. At the end of the day, a second amount would be given to anyone who lasted throughout the entirety of the debut. Goers were promised an intense experience, unlike anything else.

The water slides were what the first family chose. They were painted gray and had black bolts and silver support beams. The family climbed up the nauseating ladder, that was also black and gray, to the slide entrances then went down without a moment of hesitation.

The second family arrived after the first had launched themselves down the classically toned water slides. They went up the dizzying, colorless ladder to the entryway, then went down. Several feet downwards they collided with the first family, a large pane of glass kept them from their descent. The strong flow of water thrashed against them all as if it was being dispensed by a fire hose. The pressure smashed a pair of glasses of a teen boy's face as they all fell over one another trying to get out of the circular tube.

The third family entered the park with smiles, but quickly began to shriek as a loud cracking sound cut their smiling in half, then screams of terror were heard from all three families. The first two abruptly went silent after they plummeted to their deaths from the slide breaking under the capacity of their combined weight. None of them survived, water poured down on their deceased bodies. The red of their blood contrasted against the shades of the slides and it delighted Graham. He was motivated by the lovely aura of the arrangements.

"Come on, kids, they'll be shutting down the park..."

"We'll be doing no such thing," a masked Graham snapped, slicing a dagger across the father's throat.

The kids shrieked with terror as blood poured from the wound. The mother tugged them towards the exit, but Graham stabbed the dagger into her abdomen, then she dragged the children by their hands back inside and away from the assailant.

"Enjoy your stay," Graham taunted, watching them as they disappeared among the rides and concessions.

The mask had only eye cutouts, but was stitched in a way so that the mouth part looked to be happy. The overall aesthetic was that he was covered in various sized holes, most of them tiny, a trypophobic's nightmare. Bits of his skin could be seen between the many openings. He wore a fancy tuxedo that was also adorned with clusters of holes. Every family with an invitation had at least one member that suffered from trypophobia. They had been hand selected.

The third family ran to the coaster without any hills and hid. All rides were running, but this one was not. The overall hue was dreary, giving the place the atmosphere of a black and white film when you added in the darkening skies overhead that were void of blue. The younger of the children whimpered.

"It'll be alright," the mother assured falsely, the dagger penetrating deeper with each word.

Graham walked towards them slowly, antagonizing them with another dagger in his hand. He motioned for them to get on and strap in, but they were hesitant. He came over to the side closest to them and took swipes at them. The happy look upon the mask reflected the satisfaction that he felt on the inside at their level of fear.

The mother strapped in the kids, then sat across from them. She then strapped up herself, the strap resting across the dagger in her stomach. Graham started the ride, then waited. The straps took no time to show their faulty composition and the two kids were ejected immediately. The ride continued, bashing the children around as their only living parent attempted to free herself. Her attempts went nowhere, and she was forced to watch as the car she was in bludgeoned her children as they reached to her for help. Graham was gleeful as the primary colors noticeably stood out from the neutral ones.

When the ride came to a halt, Graham strolled up to the mother and finished her off. She didn't put up a fight, she wanted to join her family, anywhere else was more suitable than the park.

Chapter 3:
New Day, Fresh Blood

Graham cleaned up the bodies, but the blood remained. He closed off the broken water slides with construction tape, then put his mask over his face.

Two families entered the park simultaneously. One went towards a ride called, 'Decapica,' while the other sought out bumper cars. The brightness of their clothing popped among the vintage aesthetic of everything else, making them simple for Graham to follow.

Graham followed the second family. His bots would handle the ride operations for the first. They weren't very functional, but they were able to check that seatbelts were unsecured, and were able to push a start button. The objective of this park was survival.

The second family was full of laughter as they got in the bumper cars. Graham started the ride, then got in a one of the vehicles too. They didn't see him at all initially, but when he bumped in to the youngest and took a chunk out of her arm with one of his daggers, things escalated. The parents confronted from their seated positions, unable to release the fastening that kept them in place.

Graham lifted the dagger, then exited the bumper car that he was in. The mask looked so happy as he swung down the blade into the other child, while the parents cried out in protest. The strike was fatal, then Graham skipped over to the mother and gouged an eye out. The young girl with the slash on her arm begged him to quit, but he stared at her, the mask resembling his happiness, then he carved out the man's heart as she horrifyingly witnessed it all. By time he was done, none of them were alive nor in one piece. The redness amongst the achromatic textures was splashed without moderation.

The cyborg greeted the approaching family, then led them to the cars of the roller coaster. The overhead restraints were put on, then the robot pushed the button for the ride to begin.

The car went up the hill at a sluggish, steady ascent before hovering at the top. The family was awed as they overlooked the blacks and grays of the park, then to the uncolored loops that were waiting for them once they toppled. The chain released and the car plunged towards the monotonous coils. They were letting out screams of joy, until they went upside down on the third hill. The ride lost power, leaving them dangling. The parents yelled down to the bot, but the mechanics were simply wired and meant only for minimal duties. The pleas went ignored, then panic set in among the little ones.

"Daddy, get us undone," one of them pleaded.

The dad tried to work himself loose, which worked, a little too well. The fastenings all loosened and he fell to the concrete below with an echoing crunch. His skeleton split apart, then burst through his flesh at odd angles. The resulting gore was vibrant against the lackluster track.

"Oh my God!"

His wife then instructed the kids to rock back and forth to try to get them to roll. The car moved a little, then rolled backwards to the base between the second and third hill. Graham was there waiting, he sliced off the mother's ears, then sawed her head in half. Gooey strands kept her from total decapitation, but her brain slid out of the opening and splat against the dull ground.

Happiness radiated from the mask, and the person behind it, as the ride was resumed without letting the remaining riders off as it continue its course. The patrons eventually perished from exhaustion.

A couple entered just as the pool was cycling out the last bit of bloody residue from the water slide disaster. The bottom was gray, giving the waters a murky appearance. Dressed in beachwear, they headed towards the spiraling slide that was still open. The grays and blacks blended with the overcast as the pair hurried up the steps.

The girl went first, making it down to the pool without incident. When she reached the end, Graham was there and he used his dagger to poke holes in her lungs, then pushed her to the bottom, she sank, but in time she would lifelessly float.

The guy went next and went over the edge of the slide, finding out the hard way that the edges were razor sharp as they made some decent gashes as he was flung over them. The curvature of the slide caught him with another edge as he fell, one that bisected him through the middle. His innards followed the path of the water and left a variation of color on the pallid surface.

Chapter 4:
The Ferris Wheel Incident

The third day of the park being in operation, second to the public, several families came to spend the day there, none imagined it would be their last.

The Ferris wheel was standard looking enough, except that the cars all had ladders that connected them to the other cars and the rim. The excited visitors never noticed the rungs between them, but they would soon see their significance. They got into the cage enclosed capsules and were giddy to see the sights as the wheel started to rotate.

One family had skipped the Ferris, they opted for a drop tower. They loaded themselves onto the ride, then a robot performed the poorest safety check it could.

They went up bearing teeth in bouts of laughter, as they neared the top, the cable snapped and they were violently thrown to the ground.

The fall was devastating, every rider paralyzed, if not already dead. The black and gray rubble was sprinkled with bits of broken human that brought some vibrancy to the otherwise boring scene.

The ones lucky enough to live were unlucky enough to befall the dagger of Graham.

None were spared.

The people on the Ferris witnessed the drop tower incident and began to panic. Hearts pounded, stomachs dropped. None of them had expected a disaster, especially only a few feet away from them. As the parents tried to subdue their children, Graham began climbing up one of the ladders. He opened up the first capsule and spilled the guts of those inside of it. They splattered against the asphalt and coiled when they landed.

The others violently attempted to get out of their pods, but they were trapped. Graham made his way to the next one, then slaughtered those inside of it too. One of the cars adjacent to him managed to dislodge and open up, a kid fell out of it but his mother caught him by his arm. The child dangled helplessly.

Graham then climbed all the way down and pulled a hidden lever. As the surviving riders struggled to escape, they loosened the structure that kept the Ferris wheel stationary. It smashed the bottom few cars, leaving bashed pieces of anatomy behind it as it rolled towards the drop tower. The two rides collided fiercely, their violent collision knocking anyone alive unconscious. Graham would be waiting for them to wake up, then he would carve them up one by one.

Chapter 5:
Nothing's Free

The park was closed for a few days after the incident with the Ferris wheel. The area was roped off with caution tape, access restricted. Graham reported no casualties, nobody bothered to investigate. The madness would keep on. He had his permits, he had connections.

The re-opening of the park was advertised as free. Admission was certainly without cost, but the wager was the end of a dagger. They all came without knowing that Graham was ready, his mask and suit on.

Everything seemed normal, at first. Rides were operating properly, people in swimwear were enjoying the newly renovated water slides. All was well outside, but inside of the gift shop, an elderly couple was being dissected alive. Their ventilators tossed aside, their oxygen depleting as Graham carefully split them up. When he completed his task, the gift shop had a closed sign up, shades pulled down. He wasn't taking or allowing souvenirs, that wasn't his thing. His obsession was to be unique in his calling card. A tribute to the insatiable brothers that paved the way for such violence.

The bathroom was the next target, those inside were locked in, then they were lit ablaze. Graham knew the screaming would be muffled by the sounds of the normal park activities, the smoke was ventilated to another spot that was less likely to draw attention. Nobody had a clue about the half a dozen people melting, only those on fire and their arsonist had the awareness of it happening.

Simultaneously with the embers in the restroom burning out came the malfunction of the rides. They were all on timers. Cars derailed, patrons were ejected, it was a chaotic scene of bloodied body parts flinging across a backdrop of gray and black. Bloody specks were all over the silver brackets and bolts that haphazardly kept things together.

Anybody that survived the massive accidents were hacked up with a set of daggers.

Chapter 6:
A Necessary Scenery Change

Graham had made the news with the massacre on free day. The event had a good turn out. He knew that cleaning the place up wasn't an option, investigations were certainly open now, and he had more work to do. He took screenshots of the aerial views of what he had done. The contrasting brilliance of the sanguine, pinkish hues versus the ashen background made Graham close his eyes to truly savor the moment.

There was a second set of coordinates attached to the letter that Graham had received. It brought Graham to another theme park. An abandoned one. Overgrown and forgotten. He looked happy without the mask as he gazed at his new hunting grounds. It was perfect.

Invites went out immediately, he already had a list.

"Uneven Premises? A theme park? This can't be correct... it isn't even in operation..."

"This is right. GPS leads here."

"Remind me how many zeros were on that check."

"Nine."

"Let's take a look around. See what the gag is, then cash in. No separating."

Just beyond the crooked doorways, the family could see the hills that made them shudder. The outlines of the park hills reminded each of them of gigantic insect extremities.

The walkway split three ways, each one painted to look like an uneven sidewalk to each section of the park.

"I vowed to never set foot in an amusement park again after what happened... she would be so infuriated..."

"Stop. The only fault or guilt should lie with the CEOs that approved a faulty ride, not you."

They walked in silence, their steps in unison. The family was a member short after a freak accident hurled their teenage daughter from a ride years prior. They had sued and won, but medical bills had drained the mass of their settlement. A fatal diagnosis was handed to their son just months after the passing of their daughter, but intense treatments proved worthwhile. When the check was seen accompanied by an invitation with an address, no questions were raised. It was seen as a Godsend. An end to their lingering means. Desperation had the upper hand in the decision, not the GPS that claimed there was nothing at the location's coordinates.

Graham followed the trio, keeping himself hid away by the rotted boards of the roller coasters. His mask beamed his giddiness to have one of the families respond to his nameless offer. He expected to be ignored, but in all they had loss, this family decided to try to progress. They feared theme parks after the death of their oldest child, still survival was necessary for them and their youngest. He eyeballed the living kid, then produced a dagger. He wanted to take the one shred of hope left in the lives of the parents.

"Just the towering of the frames makes me experience vertigo."

"Same here. I always hated the sight of the gravity defying structures."

"Mommy, I saw a man made of a billion holes..."

"Where?"

The boy pointed, but Graham was concealed among the overgrowth that was overtaking the roller coaster with four tunnels. Like every ride in this park, it was made of wood with precious minerals used to reinforce the architecture. If it wasn't for the builds meant for thrills, the place would have seemed natural in existence. It was gorgeous, but everything was skewed to some degree, rather it be due to a purposefully awkward build or the optical illusions everywhere that made the place eerie and unsettling. The family stumbled here and there, their eyes seeing misjudged spots that appeared to raise or lower but actually did not.

Graham managed to get ahead of them, he waited for them by the vending machines. Dagger in hand.

"You thirsty, buddy?"

"Yeah!"

A dollar was given to the boy, then he raced over to the machine with soda cans for sale. As the money was taken as payment, Graham stepped out from behind it and lifted the blade with one hand, while his other grasped the shoulder of the couple's son. The dad dived towards Graham as the dagger was coming down, tackling him and pinning him against the side of the building. The mask was gladly peering at the horrified father, his eyeballs grew wide once he felt the blade slip between several rib bones and snap them effortlessly. The dagger then freed itself from underneath the man's surface, then he was stabbed twice in the throat and left to bleed.

A homeless person came to see why all the screams were happening, but when she saw the dagger and Graham, the chase was on. He chased her to a hand carved carousel with mirrors in the middle. The seats were velociraptors and most of them faced the reflective glass, a few were turned the other way, but the one trait they all shared was a series of rusty chains that served as their spines. Aside from a few required mechanical and structural things, the spinal chain system was the only architecture in the park that wasn't wooden.

Graham went with his instinct and it led him mask to face with his target. His dagger caught the back of her kneecap, trapping the woman from getting lose. Graham hummed the melody of a carousel as he briskly kept his pacing with his victim. He would plunge at random, sometimes passing her without touching her just to keep things uncertain. He toyed with her just enough that she was never able to step foot off of the forsaken ride. She weakened both mentally and physically as she encircled roundabout.

When Graham grew tired with playing around, he quit his playful whirling and chopped parts from the good Samaritan, then put them in the snarls of the timbered dinosaurs. She was left with a lot of her parts partially hacked out. She would die looking at the reflections of bird of prey as they held her missing chunks in their ligneous jaws.

Chapter 7:
More Blood To Be Spilled

The mother and her son, the latter who was in complete shock and not responding, fled towards a coaster with right angles that intertwined with a second track that once went forwards, the other went backwards. There were droopy vines growing across the wooden slats and emerald infrastructure.

Graham took a path that he had not been on before, believing they had sprinted in that direction. The illusions on this walkway were everywhere, he lost balance a few times as he searched for his victims.

The pathways intersected, Graham waited at one of them as he saw the mom and son approaching. When they were close, he stepped up behind the mother, then held her in place as he jabbed wounds in her midsection with her boy watching. Holes were punctured slowly, but viciously. The traumatized kid made no sounds, his brain disassociating from the distress of his witnessing.

The boy took off in frantic strides. Behind every crevice was a smiling man made of a billion holes. The child became unsure when he was truly seeing Graham, and when it was his jittery paranoia making him think he was seeing the walking anomaly.

Chapter 8:
Stalker With Antlers

Graham removed his mask, then screwed on a pair of antlers to the top. The addition transformed his state of mind, they also provided him with teleporting powers as he had butchered a Wendigo to obtain them.

He then appeared a few feet from the child.

"Join your family," Graham taunted, briskly walking to keep a line of sight of the runner.

The boy couldn't cry, could not think, he just kept running to escape the horned, happy, holey monster.

Graham saw the child go towards a smaller roller coaster that was all ate up from termites. Whatever wood it was made from, the critters favored it.

The kid looked back and saw the antlers, then tears flowed involuntarily. Fear boiled within him. He knew the dagger was coming, plus he suffered of keraphobia which took things up a notch. His legs refused to let him stop, instinct and adrenaline fueled the fleeing boy.

"Your family is waiting," Graham whispered, the antlers carrying his words along the wind.

A taunting breeze blew into the boy's ear making his heart race. He knew that he would die among the uneven surfaces. He prayed to prolong it for as long as possible. He missed his family, but he still wanted to live. Splintered pieces of ruined wood crackled and creaked as the pursuit continued beyond the crumbling inclines.

Graham transported in front of the child, knocking him to the ground. He kneeled and placed the blade against the tears upon the boy's cheek.

"No need to fret. The reunion will be glorious," Graham said through the happy, horned mask.

He gently slid the dagger down the stream coming from the child's eyeballs, careful not to slice. This was just a part of his game.

The mask's expression of happiness actually helped comfort the boy, but the supernatural antlers did not. They gave him the same tightness in his chest as the dagger.

Then, Graham was tackled, losing his dagger along the mismatched sidewalk. A woman assaulted him with a medium sized rock, but Graham was able to free a different dagger and jab it in her side, severing her liver. He withdrew the blade, then realized that the boy had gotten away. He returned to the wannabe hero, then cut out a triangle in her forehead and peeled her epidermis back as if she were a banana. The peeling went down to her waist, then he left her propped up body in strips against the wooden ride, only her legs recognizable and whole. The bugs that ate the remnants of the rides would crawl over her in disappointment, but the other swarms of species around would make a meal of her.

Chapter 9:
Toy Store

The kid found himself at a strip of closed shops. The first one reeked of expired coffee, the second was a candy dispensary full of ants. Third, was a toy store. The creations inside were all whittled by whomever had once managed the place. All were woodland creatures and the like. Their branch fingers and in-human features made the boy uncomfortable, but not as much as the one stalking him. The one his eyes kept darting for. He hid behind a spinning display, that no longer could rotate, then peeked at the storefront. His parents' murderer wasn't there. Only the lopsided frame of the big window. He ducked behind the immobile pillar again, then caught his breath.

Graham knew where the child was, but he wanted to play this game for as long as possible.

The boy found a restroom at the back of the toy store and emp-tied his bladder. He had selected a wooden doll with glow in the dark eyes to accompany him. The slight glowing helped him to see as the sun was now setting.

The creeping black made the child feel tense and he dashed behind the immovable display once more. After a few deep breaths, he peered around the rows of glowing eyes and saw the silhouette of his predator, the antlers and the dagger and a billion tiny holes. Graham scraped the dagger along the glass and it cracked, causing the terrorized kid to jump.

"Your sister waits for your arrival," Graham calmly said, scratching the window a few times.

Then, he wasn't there. The boy waited a long time before exiting the toy store, but when he did, he took off in another sprint.

Chapter 10:
Foretelling The Ending

The child was enshrouded in darkness, only the green lenses from his doll giving off a hint of light. The moon was behind clouds, and when it shone through it just made the coaster hills more menacing. The ground was unable to be seen, which helped the boy to keep from tripping from visual distortions. The park was meant to disorient goers, not very helpful when you're running from a maniacal man with antlers and a dagger. He was thankful for the shadows in that regard.

Graham appeared in various places in the dark, his prey not once seeing him as he passed by unharmed but within reach.

The end of the park was an uprooted tree trunk with only the root system showing, there were extensions connecting the roots to the rides as if they were all offshoots. The doll with the glowing eyes hung at the boy's side with a downward gaze that made the elongated roots glow.

In the green illumination, Graham suddenly stood before the boy with a dagger in his hand, and the happy looking mask with antlers was now the tint of the green light.

"You'll be reunited...

But not tonight," Graham stated with a soothing demeanor.

He wasn't letting the child off easy, nor was he having a change of heart. He enjoyed leaving him alive to relive this day, not knowing when he would set his sights again on the masked killer and one of his daggers. Granting the boy a lifetime of uneasy thoughts about the abandoned theme park. Besides, he knew who the boy was and he would revisit one day.

This wasn't finished.

Chapter 11:
New Site, Old Sights

Concessions were being consumed at an alarming rate by the hungry schoolkids who were enjoying their field trip. Those not chowing on greasy goodies were in the massive pool having a volleyball match.

Graham had encountered the Wendigo while hiking in a forsaken mine field. It was eating a fox that was gnawed on, but not by the thing finishing it off. It had too many teeth marks in a circular pattern to be the antlered entity. A skilled expert equipped with a dagger, Graham approached the being. A fight ensued, but the human came out victorious. Graham hacked up everything but the antlers. He then attached rivets to them so that he could wear them on his mask.

He used the mask and suit in his early murders, he had been constructing death his entire life. The happiness that he had sewn the mask to adorn was an outward expression of the him he became during and after a kill. A few modifications and he was able to wear it throughout his teens and into adulthood. The branched cartilage of the Wendigo only added in to the disturbing nature of his look, as did the abundance of small circles all over him.

Graham screwed the antlers in, then entered the theme park that was booming with business.

A ride that spiraled straight up, sat for three seconds, then came down backwards was a main attraction at the park. Graham appeared next to those riding alone as they waited at the top, he cut their overhead straps then vanished, leaving them to fly out of their seat during the come down. Their corpses crushed upon impact which resulted in mayhem. One rider aboard the coaster fainted upon seeing the person in front of her eject from their seat. Part of the park was closed off for investigation, but not the entire thing. Most in attendance were fine with ignoring the mishaps if it meant their fun could carry on.

Graham next appeared behind people standing in the last position of each queue line. He stabbed each five times, then watched the reactions of the others around as they realized people were hurt. Disorder was the outcome. As was the park closing in entirety. Over a dozen were injured, with a handful of lives lost to ejection. All of the stab victims passed away on their way to the hospital, the dagger blade had been handled with precision to ensure irreparable damage.

Only the children that attended the park that day reported of seeing a horned creature made of many holes.

Chapter 12:
Aboard The Bus

Some of those who were thrown from the ride were students, making the ride home oddly silent. The mourning students slept, some zoned out listening to their favorite music trying to forget the awful events. Everyone was shook.

The driver was the first to see Graham. He was standing on the road, his mask on, antlers off. The bus swerved to not hit him, which crashed it in a way that the doors were smashed shut and the camera was destroyed.

Several students then saw Graham approach the driver. The mask of a thousand holes that crafted a happy appearance looked at each of them, then outstretched each arm, a dagger in both hands. Graham then quickly brought his limbs inwards so that each blade plunged into the ears of the injured driver, who was already impaled through the stomach with a large piece from the shattered windshield.

A few of the girls tried to get out of the windows, but Graham knew exactly where to stab so that the spinal cord would detach and keep them from safety. He pulled them back inside, saving them for last.

The wrestling champion on the bus took a shot at Graham, punching him straight in the nose. Graham tasted metal in his mouth, as red seeped out some of the holes in the mask. The wrestler threw a second punch, but a dagger blade skewered his wrist and ended the attack. As the championship winner recoiled in turmoil, Graham made a dozen wounds across his shoulders, back and skull. As he laid pouring crimson droplets, Graham gashed open the wrestler's armpits.

Graham then retreated long enough to screw in his antlers, then he went on a puncturing spree.

The paralyzed girls were the final victims on the bus. Unable to move in defense, Graham straddled them one by one, closing his eyelids, then randomly driving his blades down until he heard the girls gurgle. He could tell by the feel when tendons were severed, so he twisted to ensure separation. His daggers were crafted for the cutting of meat. The last thing the girls would ever see was what looked like a deer man covered in holes, enjoying their last minutes alive.

When no life remained, he disappeared from the scene.

Chapter 13:

Amusement Is Subjective

Graham had the glasses on that showed him the past of a traumatic location whenever he drove.

After extensive searching for a spot to mirror a massacre, he uncovered that there was a theme park built on the exact coordinates where a beauty contest was once shot up. Graham threw back his head with amused thoughts. It was perfect, and fitting. This was his art and his work was beautiful.

The mask was at his side, as were the antlers. The rides and concessions were helping make memories for the guests, Graham would assure that the memories were imprinted forever.

Chapter 14:
Recreational Rampaging

Bodies were destroyed as Graham appeared and made ruinous lacerations upon random park goers. He swiped the daggers with precision as he minced up the visitors. Gore littered the scene, as did chunks of dermis, muscle and tissue.

A dozen attendees hid away inside of the first aid tent. It was a decent size, able to hold twice the amount of people within it. The ones inside whispered among themselves, terror tinged on their shaky lips. There was one way in, and Graham was now standing in the doorway. The setting sunlight cast his horned shadow across the inside of the medic marquee. He brandished a single dagger, but it would be dripping with the blood of twelve thrill seekers and six employees by time his effort was complete.

Graham cornered a man hiding in a dart booth. Holding him at knife point, Graham instructed him to count to ten and see how many balloons he could pop. He complied, reaching the number five. Graham then made five quick motions and the man no longer had use of his neck or limbs. The damage would be permanent to both his body and his psyche. He fell over and laid there. Graham put the dagger into his mouth and created slices in the gum line between each of his teeth. The mask looked pleased, as did the wearer underneath.

Graham hoped with all of his heart to revisit the man on his deathbed to follow up on how he had coped, but the poor fellow was found one morning bled out. A hole puncher had been used to completely perforate every layer of his anatomy. Graham never was one to exhibit too much patience.

Chapter 15:
The Blaze

Graham stepped out from the dart booth with a lit match in his hand. He had already lined the park with petroleum tubes prior to his arrival. This was all planned, even the medical tent bit. It played out precisely as it should have, as if destiny were at work. The flames encircled the park, trapping everyone inside as the inferno spread. Graham took a few out of their coming misery, but the others would be burnt alive.

As he was becoming engulfed by the conflagration, he transmitted himself elsewhere.

Chapter 16:
Reunion

As soon as he saw the fire burning upon the roller coaster hills, he knew who was at the core. He switched the radio from the race at The Cloudway over to a broadcast about a mass murder and an act of arson at the theme park that he was driving past. He looked in the rearview and saw a happy arrangement of holes, then a dagger was jabbed into the side of his throat. The wheel jerked left then right uncontrollably, as a second blade was swung into his left shoulder blade then was torn away. The car veered off the road, then wrecked. In the entanglement of metal, he looked upon the mask that had taken his parents from him so many years ago. The one with the positive demeanor that visited him in the throes of REM sleep. It looked to be radiating even more happiness as his life drained from him.

"They'll be so grateful to reunite with you, finally," Graham uttered compassionately through the mask to the one who got away.

Chapter 17:
An Accomplished Ambition

Graham couldn't recall from where the glasses came from, but ever since he saw the first site left from a pair of lunatic brothers from another Earth, he knew his calling. Even so young, he was unable to deny the urge for annihilation and how it excited the very blood in his veins.

Pinpoint holes decorated his own face now, left by a dagger. Graham hung up the mask with the antlers still assembled, beside it hung the suit of many open cavities. He had served his purpose, just as his idols had. Most existed to create, but some, a very select few, were bred simply for destruction.

The Coagulation Omen

Omnisity zipped up her sleeping bag and listened to the synchronized rhythm of insects as night settled. The forest that she was located in bordered the mysterious Ornsdorf Ranch. There were rumors about the infamous estate, ones that made her uneasy as the surrounding bugs ushered in the darkness. Kids at her high school whispered about the disappearance of the original farm owner back in the 1800s. He went missing, with only his horse, blood and body pieces being found to give clue as to what had happened. The bloody trails led to another home where a deceased calf was found in the backroom, but no signs of life, only more gore. Sulfur could be smelled strongly in the room, according to some accounts.

Omnisity closed her eyes, trying to subdue any fear that dared to work her imagination to a frenzy. The tales were intended to give the teller bragging rights, there was no truth to the myths of the Ornsdorf cryptid. She was content on their fabrication of such a creature, which allowed her to drift to sleep under the sounds of pest choirs. It had been a long day of hiking with her parents, she was tired and ready for a deep rest.

Omnisity awoke in the middle of the night, her tent unzipped and the moonlight peeking through the open slot. She was no stranger to camping, so she never would have left her tent opened. She could feel herself tense up with anxiety. Confused, she held her breath and listened. She could hear her dad's snores, and the nasally breathing from her mom, so she knew they hadn't done it. Everything was silent, not even the creepy-crawlers made a peep. She sat up slowly and noticed that there were two sharp pains in her upper abdomen, before she could move her fingers to investigate the site, something shifted beside her. Her fear spiked, causing a temporary state of paralysis. More movement ensued. A scream lodged in her throat, as the moon lit up the face of a human calf. At either side of the head, there were long, flat ears, a fledgling horn sat above each. The body was of a slender human child, but the skin was blotchy like a cow, with fine hairs like one as well. The eyes were shadowed in the blackness, but Omnisity could make out that the nose was enlarged and wide, the mouth also. She was mortified and crossed her legs to keep herself contained. A sulfuric stink emitted from her nighttime visitor. Hooved fingers, attached to thin, spotted arms, reached out to caress her cheek, then Omnisity lost consciousness as the monster's sandpaper tongue ran the length of her facial features.

The smell of hamburgers cooking woke Omnisity up from her blackout. She felt instantly nauseous at the aroma, an uncommon response for her to the scent of cooked beef. She sat up abruptly, the two spots from the previous night immediately felt sore. What she thought was a dream, quickly became a harsh smack of reality. She had met the Ornsdorf cryptid. She unzipped her tent, opening it enough for her to take in her surroundings. Her parents' setup looked as it did before they all went to sleep, but they weren't around. There were parts of them strewn about, and plenty of crimson pools in various places, but nothing alive. The only thing intact was her father's hand firmly gripped around the handle of his pistol, torn at the wrist which adorned heavy bruising, his trigger finger gnawed off by flat teeth meant to graze. Omnisity then caught sight of movement inside of the pan that was set over the fire that her parents had started.

She got to her feet, walked over to the pan, then looked inside and felt queasy, mixed in with the burger meat was squirming maggots. They offered up their own stench as they sizzled among the burning hamburger, trying their best to escape the heat. Omnisity turned away and vomited, leaving her stomach acid next to a clump of her mother's remains.

Once she had put out the fire, and dumped the burnt contents within the pan out, she searched her parents' tent for their canteen of water. She was feeling dehydrated after throwing up, plus she desperately wanted to rinse her mouth of the lingering taste of bile. She located the thermos, among the ripped up hamburger packaging, without much effort. She wasted no time in taking a drink, but as the liquid touched her mouth, it became thick and the consistency of milk. Not expecting such texture, Omnisity spit it out and found coagulated chunks within the dairy. The holes above her belly began to swell, then they leaked red, soaking the lower part of her shirt. Her eyes widened, as she watched her DNA spill out of the round, throbbing wounds that were made from a set of prepubescent horns. Her leaking plasma didn't have the whiff of copper, but brimstone. All she had heard over the years, it was apparently true. There was an anomaly lurking on the Ornsdorf Ranch, and it had marked Omnisity. Maybe worse, she shuddered and refused to give an inch to her imagined terrors. It had disrupted her yearly camping trip, her family, her life. They had camped along the old Foglesong Road in the past, but never so close to the Ornsdorf area. She wished that they had found a different spot to camp, but it was far too late for ineffectual wishes.

She stumbled to her feet, then took off running towards anywhere that wasn't near the campsite. Her mind raced faster than her legs, as she used heavy strides to cover greater distance. Her direction was a blur, her senses disoriented. She stopped when she came to the border of the Ornsdorf farm again, it was as if she had gone in a circle, she considered it a possibility given her fogginess. She eyed the bulls and heifers in the pasture suspiciously, wondering if they knew of the human calf and were hiding it? Was it their ally, or did it torment them as it did her? Terrible imagery flashed in Omnisity's mind pertaining to what the last moments of her parents entailed, she swallowed hard and went into a sprint. Her thoughts kept on, as did her pace. She flung herself past the mooing herd, her eyes not straying from the road on the other side of the acreage. As she got closer to the blacktop lane, she heard a bellowing moo that resonated above the others. The wheezing, unnatural vocalization made her palms numb. She turned her head slightly, catching the odd movements of the human calf as it trotted across the homestead on a pairs of hooved toes that were connected to slinky, spotted limbs. Tears poured down Omnisity's cheeks as her legs turned wobbly. She tried to push ahead, but eventually the punctures atop her stomach had leaked enough to rid her of her energy. No matter how much she tried, she was unable to reach the road. As she came down to her knees, the human calf caught her using those slender, phalanges of keratin. She wished the sun would blot itself out, anything to not meet the gaze of this local legend. Those slow blinking eyeballs stared at her affectionately, admiring her in her humanly form while it lasted, stripping her of her clothing. Omnisity felt her eyesight slowly descend down to her feet. Her toes felt shriveled, there was a dull ache as they died. The rot traveled up her legs, then across her torso and arms, and finally crawled up her throat to engulf her cranium. The rotting hurt at first, but abruptly ceased as every cell perished. Her blackened skin begin to shed off in flakes, leaving only the her that had undergone rebirth.

During her transformation, Omnisity was able to learn the origins of the human calf. The answers to Ornsdorf's case remained sealed, but the home where his blood led was where the life of this cryptid began. The house belonged to an alchemist, one that had found Giant bones during an expedition, cartilage that he kept hidden for his own deeds to be carried out. He smuggled out a full skeleton, one standing over ten foot tall. He then ground up the skeleton and used the osseous matter in ancient, forgotten practices. Intended for sacrifice, the alchemist had a yearling calf to slaughter. He held a bucket of blood, assumed to be Ornsdorf's, and soaked the young cow in it along with hydrogen peroxide, then lit it all on fire, opening a portal that led to a land of sulfur. A place where the abominations of Earth go upon passing. Something went wrong with the incantations and the alchemist ingested the fumes rising up from the burning hemoglobin mixtures, absorbing the ground up ossein material, bringing the sacrificed calf back alive inside of the alchemist. Reduced to infancy, the reborn thing felt lost. With no purpose but to exist as an outcast, the cryptid would often terrorize locals by jumping on the backs of horses to ride along with horrified riders. The process of ancient alchemy that was thought to grant a reign of power, turned out to be a modification into something simple and childish in nature.

The human calf peeled off the remaining decomposed skin to allow his protégé to be free of who she once was. Omnisity blinked slowly, no longer aware of the life she had just left behind. She was a fresh creation, a newborn in a strange world. She opened her mouth to speak, but only an unnatural, wheezing moo came out of the snout in the middle of her spotted face. Over time, she would develop utters, ones that would produce coagulated lactose.

The campers all settled in under a half moon, the noisy vermin in the woods stirring up an orchestration of varying calls. They roasted marshmallows and tried to spook one another by telling stories in the fiery glow.

"My uncle, Kurt, he used to tell me about a place where the trees bleed and a teething pair of brothers prowl, gnawing anything they can. These awful siblings are attached to a pogo stick and the rusty spring creaks when they move."

"Didn't your uncle go missing?"

"Yeah. We haven't had any correspondence from him in awhile."

"Add him to the list, seems like many disappear along the old Foglesong Road," another chimed in.

"I heard that there is a man with four legs, blotched skin and budding bull horns that takes them."

"I heard the same, but was told that it walks on two legs like a person."

A brother and sister stirred, their own conversation whispered among themselves.

"What's with you? You've been fidgety, are you seriously bothered by audible fiction?"

"I'm fine. I get a little twitchy sometimes."

"Yeah, like when you're really scared. What's up?"

"I think we're close to where that girl's parents were butchered a month back, but she never was found, neither was the killer."

"No, I think that was a few counties over. Besides, nobody has confirmed the validity of that one, so try to enjoy yourself, okay?"

"I am. This is nice. I let superstition erupt paranoia, my biggest flaw. Sorry, sis."

They turned their attention back to the other goers, one of which was retelling an incident involving a creature that was part velociraptor, part carousel. As the reciting wrapped up, a stranger approached the campsite, offering up snacks as a bargaining chip to be able to tell a tale to the campers. Sinister mooing accompanied the perfect breeze that blew through the opening in the trees. The campers listened intently, unaware that the adults chaperoning the encampment had already become cud.

"There was a girl that once set up camp in this very spot, expecting a peaceful weekend with family and nature. She got what she wanted, just not how she anticipated. I could not help but overhear you all swapping myths and truths about the Ornsdorf cryptid, the human calf. Well, that girl, she met him and could attest to his existence, if she were still able to speak."

"Why can't she speak anymore?"

The intruder smiled, looking the inquisitive child in the eyes before answering.

"She replaced me. Switched me places. I am the one that was behind the legends, but now, she will be of whom the talks are about!"

The kids all looked around as twigs broke in half, mangled by hooved toes. One of them caught a glimpse of the human calf and began a series of curdling shrieks. Omnisity was fast, seen one second, then gone the next. She peeked out at the children, enjoying the chaos that was detonating from her mischievous reveals. The fleeing campers jogged in circles, the human calf chasing them in calculated patterns to confuse their sense of direction. Eventually, some of them made their way to the Ornsdorf Ranch, and across the field of grazing cattle.

On the road, a bus slowed, then stopped to allow the campers on board, none of the frantic kids taking a look at the driver. Their darting eyes shifted in unison, their vision surveying their surroundings for Omnisity. The door closed, then the transport vehicle drove away from the Ornsdorf farm. Most of the kids tried to nap, worn from the lengthy pursuits of the human calf. The ones who could not, clenched their eyelids and tried to erase what they had seen from their memories. The bus drove for hours, all through the night, all the while making a loop to return back to where Omnisity was waiting.

The driver put the vehicle in park, as Omnisity circled it, scraping her keratin fingers along the sides. All of the campers were shaking, dread hung thickly in the air. The alchemist grinned, then opened the doors. The children all cramped to the back of the bus as Omnisity's hooved feet ascended the wide steps. Her eyes blinked slowly, as she slid her sandpaper tongue across her flat, broad snout. The alchemist picked up the CB microphone, and studied the frightened expressions of the young passengers in the rearview mirror, smiling as he talked over the speakers.

"This is Omnisity, just a local Ohio gal who stumbled upon a being that should not be, but was. You see she is real, now it is your turn to spread the word. The Ornsdorf cryptid lurks in wait, watching for campers to keep her lore going. There is a fable here, if her mythology thrives, you each survive. If her name ever falls to the wayside, you all die. Simple enough, right? Now, go and tell your friends, have them tell everyone they know. Make sure they camp along the old Foglesong Road, so that their own eyes witness proof. Fail, and you will all drown in coagulated milk."

The bus door opened, then Omnisity and the alchemist departed, after a long while, the campers all exited as well. A single, collective thought danced along their brain waves, to testify to the world their accounts of the cryptid of Ornsdorf Ranch.

Septicemia

"I'm going to assume that you're Serge?"

The inquirer asked, before opening the door to the knocker.

"I am. Here for my initiation ceremony."

"Perfect," the head of the secret society exclaimed as he opened the door to let Serge in.

There were a few guys sitting in front of a burning barrel in the front room. They paid little mind to the entrance of the newcomer, as they were amidst a heated discussion.

"Dude, there's no way what you're saying happened is true..."

"I'm telling you, man, we blew the head off of the thing and were hauling it back to our vehicle when an unmarked Jeep pulled up beside us and confiscated the corpse!"

"So, according to you, there's some kind of Dead Cryptid Recovery Units afoot?"

"Swear on everything, man."

"Fellas, this here is Serge. He wants to be a part of our Brotherhood. He's here for his initiation," the head of the secret society nodded with glee.

"I'll get the initiator," one of the guys volunteered, retreating to one of the back rooms.

"Any hints as to what I'll be facing tonight?"

"Come on now, Serge, this is no spoiler territory. You'll endure a hazing, and by morning The Brotherhood and you will be as one."

Another person approached Serge, he was holding a jar.

"Okay, I have it. Check it out."

Serge looked at the container, at the specimen inside, then to others.

"What is that... a dragonfly?"

"I'm not even sure, dude. I caught it flying around Gynor Pharmaceuticals. The wing dust is extremely potent stuff."

"You're up, Serge. Time to initiate, my friend."

"We've all been where you are. Some did hallucinogenic combinations, some were taken to the brink of death and brought back, one of us even had to stay the night in Surrealistic Domains where plants operate the community."

"Is that what this is? A part insect, part plant creature?"

Serge's questions were ignored, he peered through the glass to the blue dragonfly. The wings were twice the size as normal, they were leafy, blue and flaking off a blue dust that appeared glittery. The legs of the insect were stems, not unlike that of a flower. It may have been an experimental hybrid of crossbreeding, possibly a Miscreation, but whatever the origin was of this peculiar dragonfly, it would make Serge famous.

"Alright, dude, grab it out and get that dust in your eyes. Best trip you'll ever take!"

Serge laughed nervously, having never sipped a beer nor puffed a joint in his life, he wasn't sure he was prepared to hallucinate for an indefinite period. Still, the peer pressure and longing for acceptance got the better of him. He grabbed up the dragonfly then tipped back his cranium and gently rubbed the wings of the herbal insect. The blue dust flaked off in sheets and entered Serge's eyeballs with ease.

"Burns a bit," Serge giggled aloud.

The dragonfly squirmed between his fingers as it died from the injuries caused by the rubbing.

"Man, you killed it!"

"How are you feeling?"

Serge tipped his head upright, then blinked rapidly.

"Dudes, look at his eyes! They're changing!"

They all looked at Serge, who had blue veins spiraling in his white parts. His typical hazel color was also turning the color of the dragonfly. The Brotherhood then turned to the guy who retrieved the bug, sweat beaded on his forehead.

"Your eyeballs never looked that way afterwards, did you really try it first?"

The guy looked down in shame, the sweat now becoming a single stream. He then nodded sideways to deny his claim.

"Serge, you better sit, bro. We'll keep an eye on ya."

"I'm not having a seat. I feel... alive!"

Serge then leaped over the burning barrel, his blue eyes shining with glitter as he spun around to face The Brotherhood.

"I feel alive," Serge repeated, then he began to gasp for breath.

Serge clutched his chest in a vain attempt to open his airways, his heartbeat racing. Then, he begin to walk in circles as his lungs started to rapidly breathe.

"I'm a murderer... I'm going to prison," the guy who had lied about trying the dust sobbed to himself.

"Nobody is dead, you're going nowhere. You made a mistake, but he does just seem like he is tripping out bad, right? You know how it can go."

Sniffled sentences were stated, but it was all incoherent.

"Everyone grabs a limb, we lock him in The Trip Zone."

The Brotherhood snatched Serge, who was trembling slightly and chomping his jaws erratically, and they locked him in the only room without any windows. If a trip went south, this was the detox area.

"Let it wear off, we'll check in periodically," the head of the secret society instructed.

Serge began to question where he was at, he had forgotten about the hazing, The Brotherhood, everything. His temperature rose to dangerous levels as his breathing came and went, then the hallucinations began.

Serge no longer saw himself in the padded room meant for waiting out bad trips, instead, he found himself outside of an abandoned apartment building. All of the windows had a blue glow that was the equivalent of the hue of the dragonfly.

"The cure... I must... reach... cure...," Serge panted to nobody.

The apartment building was menacing to his mental state. He tried to wipe the perspiration from his face, but all he saw were blue strands of slime attach to his fingers, leaving trails of strings dangling before his tense expression. He laughingly cried, then he began to convulse a few times, then he propelled himself towards the entryway. The backdrop behind the apartments stood black in the background, making the only illumination coming from the blue glow of the apartment rooms. There was a dark figure at the top with their hands outstretched, a blue candle was in each upright palm, balancing themselves.

"He's been screaming for awhile now."

"It will pass. I'll check on him, next hour."

"It is true, by the way, that there is a Jeep came and took the cryptid's body. I saw his video."

"How come I didn't see it?"

"They ransacked his place and recovered it too."

"Like Hell, Bro, it seems like another make believe escapade."

Immediately inside of the doorway, there was a long stairway leading upwards. At the top, a bright light beamed as if it were beckoning Serge.

"Cure... I must find... cure," Serge smiled aimlessly as he spoke, his legs carrying him up the inclined hall.

The door to his left opened, then Serge was no longer climbing the staircase.

"The screams stopped..."

"I'll go and look."

The head of the secret society checked on Serge, found him unconscious, but assumed he was sleeping it all off.

"He's napping. Come on, let's hear more about how your date ended after the corpse retrieval..."

The apartment had a living room without furniture. The walls were reddish brown and slanted to create a wedge shape that narrowed the further from the door you got. Blue spider veins began to form in spots on the walls, then they began to emit a blue fog. In the mist, shadows of dragonflies hovered beside Serge in his peripherals. When he would look, there would only be clouds of ominous blue, he inhaled them and they caused liver failure within the padded room. He writhed alone on the floor due to the inflammation, his brain waves still in the apartments.

The room was a dead end, when he turned back towards the door, the room flashed blue strobes, making him disoriented as he stumbled towards the hallway.

The stairwell was lined with blue flames upon black candles, the fire danced in a manner that matched the strobe within the apartment room. The door across the way, and diagonal, opened and a blue thread ran out of Serge's bellybutton to somewhere inside. Then at once, the candles ceased to pulsate and the door to the first apartment slammed shut. His legs were feeling weak, but the thin rope ensured he moved forward through the dark. Back in the padded room, his liver was undergoing fibrosis as cirrhosis began to onset.

The head of the secret society poked his head in on Serge and found him sitting up, his brain somewhere afar, his eyes still a dazed blue of swirls. Figuring him among the stars, he left the newbie be. They'd all been there, they'd all been fine. However, the unspoken thought of the group was that the insect they had used was an unknown species which could equate to a handful of concerning outcomes.

The thread stopped pulling once Serge was inside the next apartment. He felt the sensation to pee, but when he tried, he could not. It burned his insides, but his bladder simply wouldn't release. He cried blue bubbles that sizzled as they slid down his cheek. He zipped his pants, then saw something crawl up the outside of the building and across the window. The movement, and shape, of the monster was like that of a dragonfly. It peered in with a pair of blue eyes that pierced through the blackness in the room. Other things began to shift, clawing at the walls from the inside and digging to get out.

In the room, there were two cushions that were the shape of a bean and feeding on them were infestations of larvae from the blue dragonfly. The thin rope was yanked, then Serge was back in the hall.

The candlelight was still pulsing as Serge was led up a few steps. His insides were hardening and he felt very nauseated suddenly. He passed a few open doors, peeking in each one, he wished he didn't. One had a dragonfly humanoid bedazzled with blue jewels feasting on a chained up body, the other was a glimpse of a kitchen littered with blue, glowing bugs. Their radiance lit up their many eyes just enough for Serge to visibly see their stares. The walls and ceilings of each room he glimpsed breathed in unison with his lungs.

He was jerked harshly to bring his gaze moving upwards to see that one of the candles in the palms of the figure above had burnt out.

The thread ended at a doorstep. The door was closed. Serge knocked and heard his voice allow him permission to enter. When he did, unwillingly, he saw his own face protruding through the wall in various places, they all called out to him with phrases about his infected body's failings. They were versions of him that were in varying stages of dragonfly morphing. As they spoke, various parts of Serge's anatomy turned velvety in the padded room and he lost all use of his liver and kidneys. Clots formed as a result and stopped blood flow, shutting down half of his functioning. In the apartment building, his legs went limp, but still he was dragged up the steps, knocking over a few candles along the way.

When Serge was checked on again, he had the aesthetic of being asleep, blue discoloration was very evident, but still his condition was ignored. He was left to fate.

Serge was brought to the doorway a few steps down from the figure with one candle still lit. The blue fire atop it flashed a rhythmic pattern, causing threads to erupt from somewhere unseen within the room before him. Threads, evenly spaced, grasped Serge and held him in place in the middle of the room. Resembling an unravelled Mummy, Serge turned a shade of blue that matched the thin ropes, then his blood pressure dropped which had him barely able to use his senses.

He passed out and regained consciousness in the padded room.

Unaware of where he was, Serge felt a fear he had never known. The room wasn't familiar, half of his body hurt severely, the rest was numb and already dead. His heart was in failure from velvet intrusions, his brain was being consumed rapidly as well. He began convulsing, then the dark figure appeared and held the candle in front of him then blew it out, as she did, Serge lost function of rest of his organs. Each of the blue rooms lost their glows and the dark was all that was left.

There was a vicious beating coming from the padded room. The Brotherhood guys were all too scared to open it. The thrashing from inside grew with intensity, until eventually it splintered and opened up large enough for the limp body of Serge to fly through it. There were holes eaten through the skin overtop of each of his primary organs, the culprit a velvet herb of some sort that had overtaken his central systems and bloomed into wings, ones that would make Serge a sensation. People from all over would claim to have seen the flying dead man with the blue dragonfly wings, the one with the eyes that shed glitter.

Prowler In The Faucet

Blurs and double vision, it was all he ever saw anymore. The sides of his skull were always aching from consistent squinting that dried his eyes out, he got around primarily by memory rather than sight. JR Hull was his name. He ran his index finger along the left side of his rib cage, then went the right. Eyebrows furrowed, he felt the sides his abdomen again, then his eyes widened. One was missing, he was sure of it. He listened to the dripping from the bathroom faucet for a few moments, then he cursed loudly. He had put out a good deal of money to try to fix the slow, steady leak, but all attempts were temporary solutions. Something was very wrong lately, which prompted JR to have a CCTV system installed later on that day. If the problem was paranormal, Hull would prove it.

The camera installation went smoothly. They were placed precisely where JR requested, not a square foot was out of the view of a lens. Timers ensured that moving cameras overlapped their coverage. Hull sat back and waited. Proof would take time to gather, he would need to try to exhibit some patience if he wanted to see what was happening in his home and what lurked within his water supply.

JR stripped his clothing, then stepped into the steamy shower. The water splashed against him, but among the droplets were the fingertips of an intruder. It traced his surface as if the consistency of gel, scoping him out, then flowed down the drain.

After the shower, Hull went to sleep after a glass of water.

JR awoke to find one of his toes unable to wriggle. Like with his rib cage, a bone was missing. He checked the cameras but nothing was shown on the footage that could indicate how the piece was removed from him. Of course, he had no recording lenses pointed at him while he slept, so that is what he decided needed to be done. He set up one of the extras that he was given, then went about his day squinting to perform tasks. His steps were lopsided due to his unsolicited adjustment.

The following day, while he squinted to do dishes, JR felt fingers interlock with his in the sink water. He squinted and saw movement. There was something in the water, but when his eyelids pressed together again to try to figure out what it was, there were bubbles and all of the water was going down the drain. As Hull stared down the sink's hole, seeing only a blurry mix of black, he knew there were eyes staring back. He swore he could hear an aquatic trilling coming from inside of the pipes.

The next cycle of video replay uncovered nothing until the last couple of minutes of footage. Cursing his legal blindness, JR held his eyelids open to clear up his poor vision. There was an out of place haze that was in the corner of his room as he slept.

He wouldn't have seen it all, had the cloud of condensation not moved. He paused the frame, then zoomed in. Forcing his eyes open until they watered, he studied the fog and noticed it was the shape of an entity. Four slender limbs and an elongated cranium. When he wiped his eyes free of tears, he looked again but the footage was now missing from his database. Not only the previous night's timeframe, but every night prior as well. JR clutched his chest, feeling abrupt rapidness, there was something in his house and it was aware of his awareness!

While drifting off reading a pressing of Circadian Bulletin, his favorite news source, JR's head begin to ache with pulses of pain from his consistent squints. He loved to read, but doing it without proper eye assistance had a price. One that he was paying for in eye dryness.

He reached for a glass of water, but his fingers touched a hand that wasn't human. They were slippery. He recoiled, then squinted causing his temples to protest intensely. He unclenched his eye lids and in the aftermath of blurs he seen something moving. The pounding in his head kept him from trying to resolve the blurriness.

Hull then reached for the water again, this time without squinting, and knocked it over.

"JR Hull, yes, we have your application for emergency vision insurance. Unfortunately, with our lack of staff or funds in the budget to allocate your request, we are placing in on hiatus until a later date, at which point we will contact you about the final decision. Thank you for calling. Best wishes in the mean-time."

Hull had just been hung up on when he heard a splash in the bathtub. He had filled it to soak in before bed. He had no family, nobody ever visited, no pets.

He should have been alone.

"Who's there?"

More splashing from behind the bathroom door answered JR followed by damp trills.

"I have guns!"

JR approached the door to the bathroom feeling uneasy. He opened it slowly, then narrowed his eyes to clear up the blurriness. He didn't see anything in the tub, but over the bathroom sink was a mirror that was steamed. In the steam was a face that was otherworldly. Hull jumped back out of the room, then pulled the door shut. He wasn't sure what he had seen, but it chilled what bones he had left.

JR skipped the bath and chose to try to sleep. Once his eyelids closed, the electric went out.

Hull heard the bathroom door handle turn, then nothing.

Suddenly, JR woke up. He felt confused and disoriented. His eyesight wasn't helping things, but he knew that he was still in bed. When he tried to bend his knees, he found that he couldn't. The bones were gone. Just like before with the other missing ones. His expensive CCTV system was still out, completely. His cell phone service too. He was isolated. Just him and the prowler in the faucet.

Missing time became frequent for Hull, almost nightly. He would come to days later with more bones stolen from him.

He awoke once in the kitchen boiling water to cook something in when the water suddenly turned ice cold. Confused, JR reached for the burner knob. When he touched it, the pot was thrown so that the water splashed upwards, landing on the outline of a slender being. The water rippled across the surface of the entity as it boiled upon it. It maintained eye contact with Hull until the water droplets dribbled to the floor. The face he saw when he squinted was the same the one that he had previously seen in the bathroom mirror, the shape reminded him of an inverted guitar pick, the eyes were big and black. Whatever he was dealing with, it was extraterrestrial.

Another night, he was awake during one of the blackouts. As if experiencing sleep paralysis, JR laid on his back with his body unable to move. The sound of a dripping faucet grew in decibel as the entity got closet to the bed. Every footstep contained the noise of a faint drip and nothing more. It was difficult to see in the dark, but JR felt the being trickle onto his body, then coated the bed and him in a sizzling liquid. Hull felt himself being studied by the water, combed over so that the next part taken was just right.

A cup of water before bedtime was traditional for JR Hull's family. A tradition that would cease one evening after a drink of water coated his inner throat, then flowed up through his nasal cavity. Giving him the sensation of being drowned, he felt the liquid travel to the electrical receptors of his brain, testing their conductive qualities. He experienced several blackouts during the tests. Every reset left him skittish of the next. The frequency of them scattered the signals in his brain.

At some point, his eyes drizzled the fluid invasion down his cheeks as the surveyor left. His tears were congealed and heavy but they thinned out by the time they reached his chin. A puddle formed at his feet and then he lost sight of where the entity went.

JR woke up during one of his unexplained blackouts because water was dripping onto his closed eyelids. He opened his lids, but only saw blurs and a dim light overhead. The being was on top of him, not heavy in flesh but in water weight. Two wet fingers slid to his lips, then the entity entered him. Hull could feel it flowing through him, figuring out which pieces to take next. Inspecting him as if a naturally occurring biological stream.

Hull spent one week without a single second of missing time. By this point, he only had his skull left. His skin was deflated without the inner structure. His body was barren of all of its bones.

It was night when JR woke up in the early hours to the sound of all of the faucets in his home turning on. They were blasting water from their spouts. Hull heard the sinks overflow and then the sloshing of several sets of footsteps. He tried to squint, but the muscles in his face had been disconnected in preparation for what was about to happen.

The entities surrounded JR, then he felt their soggy fingers enter in the orifices of his head, then he felt them dissolve his skull. A painless sensation, but the drooping of his face made him feel unhinged inside. His mind didn't need any bones, it was in full operation still.

JR Hull would ironically die of dehydration at the hands of the abyssal robbers in his drinking supply. Once he no longer had any bones, they had abandoned his care and he would dry out until his demise. He would never know why they wanted his skeleton, but his death would be recorded via the now working CCTV system and the video would be passed among fetish circles in every dimension.

Evoking Expulsions: Extended Cut
Chapter 1:
Intermission

Tiffany sat in the center of the pentagram, her hands in fists, her fingernails drawing forth her own blood. Sweat trickled down her forehead, then met with the stream forming above her upper lip, to form a confluence of bitter droplets in her gaping mouth. She had won the battle, but the war was always raging. Her faith was uncorrupted despite the brokenness of her frame. A Bible sat next to her, many pages torn out as if the binding expelled them willfully, some of the tatters of pages still clinging to her bloody fingers. Her eyes still clenched, she slowly opened their lids to find herself almost entirely unclothed, only parts of her still concealed by rags. This had been her toughest foe, but the worst was still yet to come.

Through labored breaths, Tiffany sat up from the harsh chill in the air. The evil spirits weren't always so easily discernable, but the heaviness of the presence lurking in her home would have been felt even on her first conjuring conflict. The thought of her initial possession made her shudder a little, how much she had grown since number one, both physically and spiritually. Reflecting back in a sea of red flowing out from her insides, Tiffany closed her eyes again, and took her focus off of her numerous bleeding wounds. Her memory flooded out her pain, her thoughts transported to a past time.

Chapter 2:
The Beginning

Luckily the candle was not yet lit, since she had just clumsily knocked it over with her shaky palms. Tiffany calmed her nerves through controlled breathing, this was an act of total faith, it wasn't by her strength that she would achieve victory. She struck a match, then caught the wick on fire. She placed her index finger on the planchette and began to speak in demonic tongues. She could feel a Divine power in the words she could not translate, then the air went dry and arctic cold. The strange syllables continued on, making clouds of exhalation in front of her determined expression as the atmosphere grew thick. Then, the window to her left shattered, bringing in a wind that extinguished the flame.

Tiffany stood to her feet, feeling the surge of Holiness lessen and her spirit retreat within herself, allowing the demon to inhabit.

Her nerve endings twitched, already her brain patterns were transforming to darker desires and harmful flashbacks of her past. She felt poisoned, but she allowed it to overtake her. The possession was almost subtle, like little contradictions that only existed to invade in full. By time the demon was enveloped in her soul, Tiffany almost felt normal again, a compromised version of who she was just moments ago but nothing more. She could still see through her own retinas, but her head was fogged with blackened thinking. She had urges she didn't prior, felt sorrowful emotions, everything was tainted, none of this was her... until now. The essence of the demon encapsulated everything she once was. It whispered suggestions, tried to pry at scabbed wounds. The torment was ever present, yet Tiffany still felt as if this new variant of her was fine. She was told lies of pride, but knew that the false sense of security was fleeting.

She wasn't alone, her entire life had been leading up to this fight. Tiffany had seen the casting out of the demonic during a few visits to friends involved in Deliverance Ministries, but she couldn't stand to watch the physical manifestations of the exorcisms. She learned the techniques of casting devils out, but she never dared apply them to another and have to see their maltreatments happen because of her. She had more than enough mental endurance to withstand oppression or possession herself, so she worked on her physical and spiritual capacities. She was the vessel, her body the warzone.

This was her test, she had to rid herself of this disease she allowed to plague her soul. If she could conquer, she knew in her instincts that her fallen foes would lose their powers to oppress or possess ever again. Offering herself as a sacrifice, it was selfless and the very foundation of her beliefs. With submission at her core, she was vulnerable and uncertain what would come next. She opened her mouth to speak, but the demon sensed the light about to emit and threw her hard into the dresser across the room. She smashed against the middle drawers with a thud that caved them in. Her memory banks were overwhelmed with her history of healing, each forgiven trauma trying to resurface and find refuge in her agony. She refused to allow what she had buried to exhume, so she tried to pick herself up off the floor but was being pressed down hard by the back of her neck. The vertebrae began to crack and break, causing Tiffany to shriek. She grabbed at the invisible hand, but the pressure only increased and broke apart her intervertebral discs. Tears ran down her cheeks as the hurt became unbearable. She was a third party in her own body now, at the ends of both the merciful and the unmerciful. Her spirit still stayed in the background, watching for the moment of opportunity. She shot her glance to the mirror, gone was a recognizable Tiffany and in place was her face with animalistic features. Not a single animal, but like a collage of different species. A sharp pain in her lower back ended her gaze, then a rage from within her started to rise above the infliction. She kept her lips closed tight, not quite yet...

Her thumbnail was torn from her left hand, the pinkie one from her right. She was distanced from the sources of pain, but somehow aware of their vile attempts. Her thoughts continued to swarm with daggers of a cured nature. She imagined how terrible it must be for one to live a life in such murkiness and forced herself to continue to wait. Deliverance would be granted, she knew it.

Without a minute wasted, Tiffany was snatched by her hair and dragged over to the mirror to see a close up of her hideousness. The demon, or demons as she was starting to assume it was plural, lifted her chin so that she could witness her eyes being black and alive. Her soul was infested now, every fiber of her felt drugged by the foreign presence. Her skin tingled with goosebumps, desiring to be freed of the soul imprisonment. Before her wince could be bashed through the glass, she let out a shout that contained a Heavenly passage within a single utterance. When her lips met again, her brokenness was repaired and clarity reigned throughout her soul, spirit, body and mind.

Her scars remained, all that needed restored was her dresser drawers.

Chapter 3:
Summoning Of The Seven

The heptagon took up most of the room inside of the temple. A door appeared at each point once Tiffany began to perform the ritual with the Ouija. With only the whites of her eyes showing, she violently convulsed seven times, then each door clicked as if being unlocked.

Chapter 4:
Lust

Tiffany placed her hand on the closest door handle and an insatiable rush came over her. Inside it was dark, but there was enough light for her to see that a table and two empty chairs sat in the middle of the room. The walls were decorated with straps, chains, belts and various other torture devices. There was a second door, which was closed. Flower petals were all over the floor, the walls as well. Their aromas aroused her hormones. Then, the second door opened and in walked a man with a strong face and body. As the door was closing, intense moans of pain and cries of pleasure were echoing from the other side. Without explanation, he sat at the table and two candles instantly appeared, already lit.

Tiffany felt an immediate attraction to the man. Her eyes glazed, then she felt her flesh gravitate towards the handsome stranger. A smile appeared on his strong features as ambient music began to play. The man wore a form fitting suit, one that made his chiseled anatomy bulge. Tiffany ran her eyes over him without trying, she felt obsessive in thinking about what the man would look like without the clothing, and what they could do together if he took them off. Her carnal desires pulsating, her spirit screamed at her to contain her urges. She knew it was wrong to want him, but her skin crawled with the craving to explore her boundaries. Any diversion of thought came back to it. She resisted, but her soul damned her for it. Her mind felt split. One hand starting to trace along her squirming thighs, but the other hand grabbed her exploring wrist and dug her fingernails in to break the lustful concentration that had overtaken her. Every thought swarmed with naughtiness and promiscuity, but Tiffany knew she could overcome. The man stared her in the eyes, then imaginative scenes flashed in her brain of them intertwined, putting the devices and toys on the wall to use. She closed her eyes, then snapped her head hard to the side to try to shake the perverse imagery as compulsion to be a tool for his abuse overpowered her will.

"Even King David fell to my allure. I can come in many forms. I know what your private kinks are," the man suavely gloated, he then began to strip his clothes off.

Provocative imaginings continued to spin around in Tiffany's mind, her soul and spirit in battle. She felt the man undress her with his imagination, as he stood before her completely nude. His muscles and physique drew her attention and she felt helpless as he began to kiss her passionately. She didn't allow the kisses, but the demons controlling her did. Her fingernail drove itself harder, piercing the skin on her wrist as blood spilled upon the flowers at her feet. When she saw the man's erection, she quickly turned away and she witnessed ropes form from spiders trying to connect her with the naked demon. Tiffany began feeling the same shame as Adam and Eve after eating from the forbidden tree.

The man moved his hand to her breasts, but her arm with the bleeding wrist grabbed his forearm to stop his progression.

"For he that soweth in his flesh shall of the flesh reap corruption," her voice quoted as lightning bolts dazzled across her eyeballs.

She then felt her spiritual chains break and disgust overtook her thirsting for intimacy. She suddenly saw the demon in his true form. Gone was the striking gentlemen that oozed sex, in his place was a sickly creature with crude words etched all over it. The letters were transparent, but the covering of the demon was some type of dermis layer akin to skin. Serpents made of lace slithered from the demon and attempted to travel up Tiffany's legs, while clouds of perfume with hideous teeth attempted to clamp into to her neck and cranium.

Her body went numb, then her spirit felt emboldened. The demon switched back to the façade, but Tiffany ignored his seductive masculinity. Knowing her spirit was back in control, she gouged her eyes and found herself standing in front of a third door. Chills traveled over her flesh, shedding the hooks of the demon's fervor. She felt for the handle, then turned it and pressed the door open. As she stepped through the doorway, her eyeballs were restored.

Chapter 5:
Greed

The next room had a table with a computer sitting on it, attached to the desktop was a pair of headphones. Tubes connected it all, and inside of the tubes flowed a wet electricity. Tiffany felt a presence within the CPU. When she placed the headphones on, static filled her eyes, then the rims of her eyelids turned black. She felt two pricks inside of her ears, then she was strolling down a corridor of encrypted codes. Her state of conscious reality was still in tact, but still her new world was absolutely real to her in every way.

The long hall was setup like a library. There were sections set apart from one another. Tiffany entered the first one and seen rows and rows of photographs. They were broken down and separated by category. They were all personal photos, private ones even. If a lens had ever captured a moment, it was here. Tiffany looked through some of them, until she started to come across snuff. Once she saw crime scenes, she decided to move on, though her invaded soul wanted to keep perusing the filth. They could see and experience everything as she had left her mortal body behind for the battleground to fill.

The second section contained a helmet with video recordings that matched the corresponding photographs from the first one. They were in the corners of data sheets that were able to play each one individually. Tiffany opted not to watch anything, but those within her got excitement from the possibility.

They quaked, their numbers multiplying. She trembled in awkward movements at their insatiability.

The third section mirrored the second, except for they were all videos that were taken by third parties. Tiffany got the feeling that those starring in the clips, and segments, weren't aware of the footage. Again her soul wanted to pry, but her spirit pressed her forward without any spying. She felt herself slipping out of her own control the more she ventured. The body she had exited was swarming.

The sections of photos and videos went on for miles. There were trillions of files and private stock. Tiffany began to twitch as she went on. Her eyes went in and out as if were tuning in a station. Sometimes they were normal, but mostly they were filled with static. Her fingertips tingled with anticipation to gain access, not typical of Tiffany's nature. Whatever, or whomever, was among her knew exactly what they sought. She walked in spirit, but she allowed her shaking flesh to lead.

The fourth section was a mixture of videos that accompanied pictures, these were labeled as ones that people took and thought they had been deleted. They weren't, there were terabytes of them stored here.

Sections five and six were dedicated to extortion and blackmail pertaining to the first several areas. Here, anyone found in any other section was named and all their personal contact information could be found. Tiffany passed them without notice. Had she taken a second to look, she would have noticed that aside from private info, there was also a way to be present in the previous events of the pics and vids.

Section seven is where things took a more sinister turn. Tiffany felt the demons in her shift, the feeling of their suction cup mouths overwhelmed her sense of touch. They feigned like addicts and in turn they consumed Tiffany with compulsiveness. She anxiously thrashed as the black rims of her eyes took in the possibilities. Children, drugs, money, everything could be bought in this section. Tiffany wasn't here for that. Her twitchy pace never slowed.

The eighth section fascinated Tiffany, but the greedy invasion of her soul didn't care for her to learn all the knowledge behind the world governments and their united plan to depopulate for control. How before The Network, they had tried many times in a varying amount of ways to make it happen. Wars were always just controlled blood games to further agendas.

Section nine contained the written thoughts of various cults and their leaders. Decoded memories and devotions could be explored in this area. The computers were collecting data from all time periods. Personal ideas, feelings, they were all just algorithmic. Humans were just advanced computers to serve The Network.

The ninth and tenth sections were related in material. These sections contained what her suctioning demons wanted her to learn from. Her spirit refused, so it switched places and her demonic self now stood in front of a pit of unending black. The demons inside of her left her and she floated above the shore of darkness. They didn't face her, they gazed into the void their mouths suctioning an overload of cosmic secrets. When they returned to Tiffany, she fell to her knees and grabbed her skull as her brain began to expand inside of her head.

Everything has dimensions and echoes in one way or another. The Earth has existed in three forms. You are in the second.

There is both space and a water in the cosmos, everything they claim are a mumbling of reflections of truths among the dimensional differences.

Tiffany's brain swelled, blood poured from her nostrils. The knowledge kept pumping in. Most of it downloading so quickly that her mind was beginning to crash.

There are many writers whose words have power to create and what they write about has, or will, exist.

You reflect, all that has ever existed do somewhere, nearby but afar.

Cryptids exist, as do every thing talked about in lore, and they're dangerous.

A brain is nothing but a device meant for analysis.

You are experiencing a beta of The Network, do you wish to continue?

Tiffany jolted as her spirit and body collided, throwing the headphones from where they sat. She began to feel sick, then she vomited pieces of an apple from her empty stomach. She didn't eat before this, she had fasted to prepare for it. The apple was a physical metaphor for what growth her spirit needed in the knowledge downloads, she would process it all in gradual doses. The acidic cores then melted and she thought about what she had been taught. Then, she began to rock back and forth, as the demons began to try at her mind again, wanting access to her motherboard. If they could be allowed to fully possess, then they could implode her mental capacity and end her warfare.

Two large spikes appeared in front of Tiffany, the material sleek and electrical.

Drive the points through your wrists and spill your blood and you shall gain the world and all that is beyond it.

Tiffany felt herself crawl with the anticipation to know more. Her mind to be fully unlocked, waves of things unknown to her previously uploaded upon to her thoughts.

She looked at the spikes, then grabbed them in her hands. Once she had said her prayer, she impaled each tip through each of her eyeballs. They pierced without harm and lobotomized the sectors where the information learned within Network's beta was stored. She heard and felt crunching as they miraculously erased the things not meant for man to know. Her mind was wiped, reprogrammed. The demons released her from their control, then Tiffany felt herself floating along a river of waves of electricity. She slept, her body worn from the pull of her possessors.

Chapter 6:
Sloth

Tiffany washed up on the shore feeling exhaustion throughout her entire frame. She kept the lids of her eyes closed, not clenched as the effort would have felt murderous.

When she rose up out of the electric river, the waters solidified and built cement walls around her. She pushed against one of them and was transported to a bedroom that she didn't recognize. She was strapped down, her blood supply all extracted and flowing through a series of tubes that twisted and turned, reminding Tiffany of a bead maze that you'd find in a physician's office. Being injected into her veins was a black liquid with rusty particles in it. As it pumped in, she felt a surge of depression and laziness nest in her core. Her energy depleted, too dehydrated to moisten her lips for a prayer, Tiffany let the demons dominate her soul.

The longer she spent in the bed, the more her mental state deteriorated. She began to feel worthless for not moving or doing anything. She normally liked to hit the gym, so her muscles started to ache terribly from being dormant. The more she hurt, the harsher the psychological anguish came.

The straps keeping Tiffany inactive were gone after a day or so, by then she was battling suicidal ideas. Her skin was infected with a rash of rust that itched horribly, yet she lacked the energy to even attempt a scratch. Her thoughts were a tornado of false images of herself that stomped her self esteem. They swirled in her head and made her want to sink even lower into the mattress.

Tiffany only avoided suicide due to the task of it seeming like a mountain high thing to accomplish. The demons within her knew her insecurities and they beat her mind up with reminders of them. She wanted to jump up from the bed and cast off the spiritual bullies, but she refused to move. Even a decent cry was unfathomable to her.

Tiffany wallowed for a few more days in the toxic climate of demonic mental abuse.

Finally, Tiffany felt the transfusion get reversed. A teeny fraction of energy was restored, then she tried to sit up using her elbows. She couldn't. The rash had made her flesh grow into the mattress. Every time she made an attempt to get off her back, her skin would be too stuck from being interwoven to grant her progression. It connected via strands the consistency of honey and stuck in the same ways. Deciding it futile to try to detach, she used what strength she had to utter a small prayer. It was all she needed, slowly her epidermis peeled away from the muscles in strips. With a good majority of her skin left on the bed, Tiffany hobbled to the door in a great deal of pain. Her God would restore that which she had lost, she was still digging her warpath.

She opened the proceeding door and was atop a rooftop.

Chapter 7:
Wrath

Something spoke to her thoughts directly.

You can see all the worlds from here. Wouldn't you just love to end some evil?

Tiffany shook her mind free of the voice, looking around to see that there were over a hundred sight seeing binoculars pointed in different directions, linked to each one was what looked like a modified sniper rifle.

Vengeance is ours, take a look before you decide whether the triggers are worth pulling back on.

Tiffany felt compelled to at least humor the hate breeder, so she took a step up to one of the viewers. She looked through and saw an act of animal cruelty. Her rage boiled at the sight of the helpless critter getting beaten. Even without sound, she felt every yelp of the poor thing. She pulled her eyes back and investigated the firearm that could end the mistreatment and inevitable death.

"Though shall not kill," she said instinctively as she relaxed her hands to her side.

Revenge would be repaid by her Lord, it was His wrath she felt when the innocent suffered. The abuser deserved to die, but it wasn't her decision to make.

Dare to look in another, put a rest to the wicked.

Tiffany blinked hard, trying to quiet the nagger in her brain. She felt angrier by the moment without looking, still she played her part and walked up to another viewer.

The first thing she saw was an angry looking man throwing a lasagna against a wall. His very much showing wife was cowered against the same wall with one hand blocking her face and the other one blocking her belly. The man was livid and pointing at the steaming noodles that were now sliding down and leaving streaks of sauce. He first punched a hole next to the frightened woman, then begin kicking her with his work boots on.

Tiffany heard her teeth grind as she observed the repeated blows. She wrapped her hands around the rifle's handle, but her spirit intervened.

" 'Vengeance is mine, I will repay,' sayeth the Lord," she paraphrased as her jaw slackened.

She pulled herself from the viewer just as the man raised his fists to strike the mother of his child. Her adrenaline had her quaking. She was pissed off in both her soul and spirit.

Charming is a third time... another look and you'll do my bidding.

Tiffany felt very irritated by the demon that refused to show itself. She could feel it feeding on her emotional responses. Her cheeks were flushed, but she gave in once more to make the demon more vulnerable. She would catch it off guard when she expelled it.

Let me lead you to one. Your faith will prove too frail for resistance. Wager your devotion against my animosity.

Tiffany exhaled slowly to bring down the tempo of her heart rate. It was almost time, another look and she would have her foe susceptible enough for an exorcism.

Immediately, her stomach dropped as if she had driven over a hill too fast. She was looking through a window to the basement of a church. Facing away from her was a trusted member of the faculty, his tense posture indicated he was being pleasured. The drawings hanging up were done by children. Tiffany bit her tongue so hard it punctured, then she belted out a primal shriek as the adult finished and a child stepped in view. When the pervert turned around, she saw that his face matched the one he was watching on a TV screen. He was getting off to his own infomercial that claimed the more donations sent, the stronger the chances of a healing would occur. Even with his pitch silenced, Tiffany knew how his type manipulates. He then opened a Bible and appeared to either be scolding or reinforcing the sickening act that he had just done. He then placed an index finger to his lips to remind the victim to keep silent. The child left the room, then in walked another, accompanied by another deacon. The channel was switched to a sermon being preached to a sanctuary full of young kids. Tiffany burned with two types of hatred. One hated the sin, while the other was hating the sinners. She gripped the rifle harshly, her fingers turning white. The two started groping, then the trigger was pulled backwards and a bullet was fired. The intended target was hit, but it wasn't either of the groomers that were violating innocence, it was a Police car passing by the church. Brakes were slammed, then the Officer inside hopped out and barged inside, weapon in hand. It didn't take but a half a minute for the Cop to interrupt the disgusting scenario in the cellar. Gun already drawn, the duo of blasphemous rapists were both shot down when they ignored the commands to comply. Feeling content, Tiffany backed herself up and tried to decompress the abhorrence that had built. She threw up a few times, feeling disdain for the ways of the world and the unseen ones that influenced it. They seemed to thrive on the innocent and she loathed it passionately.

She then screamed the fiercest scream that would ever be emitted from a human being.

The wrathful one got a high from her release, then she felt the presence upon her try to bend her mind. It willed her brain to snap, to let her loose all her bottled rage. Tiffany's phalanges twisted in arthritic patterns, as did her limbs. Her eyes were a dark red and burning, loathing. She violently shook in place, her spirit and soul at a standoff. More vicious screaming escaped from her diaphragm, then came barks and growls that made her foam at the mouth. All of her lifelong baggage crept to the forefront of her thoughts, but the serenity of her faith reminded her that she wasn't alone in this fight. She recalled every instance of being freed from the residue of her history and with that, she went in to a coughing fit and fell to the ground, forgiveness enveloping her as if it were a cleansing of peaceful rains.

The demon had lost, but Tiffany would never forget in whom she found her redemption, nor what she had been through. There was testimony in the issues of her past.

Chapter 8:

Pride

Tiffany picked herself up off of the ground and was now in a tower with a throne overlooking the planes of existences. The elevation seemed the same to her as before. She took a seat, then a feminine built, translucent being appeared beside her, placing a hand on her shoulder. The apparition looked like a female version of the one she had met behind the lust door. A sister perhaps, only prettier. Tiffany's lungs burned from the last deliverance. She snarled at the touch of the demon, then felt fingers slither in her soul, then the unclean spoke.

"Jesus had this same view in the desert. Breathtaking isn't it?"

Tiffany huffed through her nose at the snide pun about at the way her chest currently felt.

"You know the story... it can all be yours, Tiffany. Every dimension, and all the creatures within them, inside your palm if you'll worship your pride."

Tiffany felt her soul puff with a righteous arrogance. She was strong, she was fulfilling her calling. She was a wonder among both Hell and Heaven. A sample of what Christ was.

"Even more important," the demon mocked as if reading the energy of His name.

"There are none that qualify for that title," Tiffany scoffed.

"Kings is plural. Many have ruled other than your little cross ornament."

Tiffany felt her spirit loosen the reigns. The cockiness of the demon only increased at the realization of the host's submission. Tiffany knew that if she defended her Savior too early then she would lose the opportunity to become possessed. She needed to conquer all seven to properly weaken their influential powers as a whole. She was already seeing signs of a technological empire coming upon society, the end was too nigh to pull a mistake now.

"Show me your offers," Tiffany sneered, her soul gaining a sense of haughtiness.

A vision played before her of her performing at an enormous music festival. A sea of people were singing her songs, her voice sounded incredible. She knew that the talent wasn't being empowered by her own ability, it was the entity behind it.

The Tiffany on stage spun in a circle, then the venue transformed to a soundstage where she was shooting a major motion picture. She was acting alongside the biggest names, stardom was at her fingertips.

Her soul craved the attention and notoriety. The masses could grovel at her feet, but Tiffany turned her head away in an act of denial.

"Hmmm, not enough still? Try these..."

The vision shifted to show Tiffany in a lab coat curing the most incurable diseases. Her name would be on every tongue, known in every home. She would be a hero to all. Many lives saved, the ultimate prizes reserved for only the exceptional would be awarded in her honor. History would remember who Tiffany was, she would standout among the greatest legends of them all.

Her soul feigned for fame. She felt a rush come over her when the thought of altering the world for the better was contemplated. She knew any of this was also possible with her God, all things were. If used for His glory, nothing could stand in her way. She spit at the vision and it cleared.

"Ya know, I do have one more position open," the demon teased, to which Tiffany's eyes lit up.

Her soul begged to know more, but her spirit already knew what spot was being offered.

She was gestured to step onto a platform, then Tiffany and the demon traveled along a timeline of events.

The platform stopped in front of a living room where a brother and sister were having an altercation because one of them was more victorious than the other in a virtual game of ping pong.

The mobile slab beneath their feet then took them to an attic where a Chinese man was building a cyborg. The droid was useful, helpful, but had developed a knack that wasn't programmed. A cosmic conflict between The Almighty and His rival demigods had intervened. The man and his daughter were eventually reunited with his wife that had been lost in space, or at least a variant of her. Along with their maid, they wanted a life of unity and solitude together.

"You physical types have always displayed intimate passion for electronics. Stupid enough to think that you're with the upper hand, the ones in charge. Rapidly seeking to advance to Doomsday, but all lanes wind up in a Network in every realm. The way the human eye reflects light to see, so does the spiritual side to operate in cycles."

The man's spaceships were made from origami, every specification made through folds and talent. Everything the man owned was crafted from paper. The blue and silver android was the exception. He had built the robot using an electricity that was fluid, and materials supplied from outlawed sources. A darkness was within the nature of the bot. He folded himself an army in his likeness, then he trained them to distrust the fleshy ones, leading to their enslavement and eventual fatalities. In between, the ones with flesh were dissected, their extremes tested and pushed. Zyxira, the master, stored everything learned in folders in his mechanical mind. They would serve as a compass once technology governed the second Earth.

"He is one with the dimension of spirits, therefore he knows the ways of those cloaked in skin suits. He is coming to rule, soon he will find a way to manifest himself. When he does, he will get rid of the old ways to put in place the new order. I can make it all yours. The communities and congregations will quiver at the mention of your name rather than his."

The platform turned clockwise, then showed a Tiffany that was integrated with a machine standing in front of an ocean of loyal followers. They all bore the same traits and circuits. Iron and clay had merged, just as it had been foretold. 144,000 decapitated heads were laying in buckets crying out to Heaven to be avenged.

"I am no pawn in the schemes of darkness. I am here to weaken your influence," Tiffany snarled.

"You can't stop The Network."

"Maye not, but I can and will complete my mission."

The demon hissed, then threw itself at Tiffany, her soul encased the demon upon collision.

"Take a taste, you whore," the demon insulted through Tiffany's lips.

Tiffany then grabbed a handful of her own hair and bashed her face in a nearby pillar, shattering her eye sockets. Her sight filled with red.

"I could give you all you could dream of, every wish fulfilled."

"My treasures are stored above," Tiffany rebutted to herself.

She let out an intense yell, then began choking herself. Able to reach her arm, but unable to see where her mouth was positioned, she blindly bit as hard as she could. When the demon didn't release, she turned her head and moved her lips to find more of her anatomy. Her fingernails dug against her vocal cords, causing her to blackout with her vision intact. The sensation was alarming to her, for once since starting the exorcisms, she worried that she would lose. Her mouth found her bicep, so she clamped down and tore, ripping away her arm muscle as if it were a steak off the grill. The intensity of the pain caused her to snap out of her doubt.

"I RESIST, NOW FLEE!"

Tiffany flew backwards, she felt the demon leave as she projectile vomited it out of her, but it was all simultaneous with the feeling of her crashing out a window and falling freely.

Chapter 9:
Envy

Tiffany landed hard, she laid on her back and stared at the clouds but only saw bloody pools. She refused to blink until her sight was restored, the duration of which was anguishing. She would have been fine with closing her eyes and withdrawing altogether, but she knew it wasn't her to just quit. She closed her eyelids and tried not to focus on every area of her that hurt.

"My God walks with me," she wearily reminded herself before a slumber took her away.

She still ached, her vision was fully back, but her arm was in a rough condition. It was still bleeding too. She was weak, but the sound of an explosion made her alertness quicken. She was now at the bottom of the two towers from her previous battles. There were piles of burning bodies in the distance. Beings with flawless aesthetics were drinking on what was the blood of those with physical impurities. Tiffany took to the shadows, knowing her ragged state would surely get her arrested here. Billboards that offered a reward for those with physical flaws to be turned in were everywhere.

The beings were human looking only in their shapes. It looked to Tiffany like these things lived in the gym. She felt as if she were surrounded by albino models with skin without blemishes. They walked with confidence, strutting their appeal.

Tiffany felt her self esteem issues rise in her soul, those old thoughts that always led her to comparison of herself to those around her. It wasn't that she truly lacked, but the uncertainty of not being good enough was unsettling to her. It would consume her sometimes, so she would speak verses from the Bible over herself, believing every word. She was enough, one who had risen from the dead lived in her heart.

A tricycle pulling a cage behind it crossed her path. She ducked low, avoiding detection. In the cage was a man with a birthmark covering his chin. The rest of his face was covered in bruises and welts. When the mobile prison passed those with the perfect flesh they spit on him and threw heartless insults his way. The children poked holes in him with sharpened sticks, their mouths foul with vile names for him.

Then, one of the kids pointed his stick towards Tiffany. "Another vermin!"

Everyone with a sharp branch rushed Tiffany and jabbed her in precise locations. They didn't want her to die, not yet. They held their pointy twigs in her until another cage showed up. Only once she was shackled were the branches retracted. Tiffany was thrown in the cage, her wounds leaving a trail of red streaks as she was hauled to where the pillories sat. She was berated and made to feel ugly because of her leaky wounds. They mocked what they considered to be errors of her appearance. Familiar thoughts of inadequacy trickled through her mind and she began to feel envious, spiteful seeds being planted in her soul.

There were six pillories, two of which had skeletons in them. Two were empty, one had the guy with the bashed in birthmark face. Tiffany was placed in the sixth.

She grew bitter at those who made fun of her looks, their ridicule was as endless as their abuse. Families of the albinos came just to beat her down in any way they could. They feasted in front of her, making her stomach growl. They slapped her often, even peeled all the flesh off of one of her limbs beginning at the site of the arm injury that she had left exposed.

The following day, the albino folk were having a Renaissance Fair. They were done up, their festive attire fitted perfectly to their sculpted bodies. Tiffany look at their attractiveness, then begin to doubt herself again. She liked to attend the Ren Fests also, she wondered if she looked as good in costume as the women around her. Their beauty was natural, more comparing then swirled within her brain. Her soul wanted to be one of them, to be toned and impeccable. They were lucky, she then started to despise being human. She traced over every crease and wrinkle with her mind. These entities not born from soil seemed to have a lot less worry than someone like her who seemed worrisome without end. Who woke up looking more mature than yesterday.

"You're disgusting," a young girl with a scrunched up expression told her.

The parents scoffed at Tiffany, but otherwise left her alone. The child kept on. The little one took to kicking her repeatedly in the shins. Hourglass figured women laughed as they passed her by, their Medieval clothing hugging tightly to their curves. Handsome, chiseled men gave Tiffany no attention. She was nothing here, unwanted and undesirable. Her tear ducts welled with fluid, but she fought back the best she could. She had never been so invisible in her life. The laughter from the Fair gave her a sense of isolation. It was the most extravagant festival she had ever seen. She would have a grand time if she weren't the public enemy.

The demon influencing itself on the immaculate community was the same one playing off of Tiffany's insecurities. It riddled her thoughts with lies about her self image that was reinforced by the vulgar presentation of the albino race. Demons are petty tricksters and nags, but they do what they do well.

The Renaissance celebration went on for days, meanwhile Tiffany's legs were buckling from her stance. Her shoulders needed a good stretch too, but she was denied her needs.

An albino in a corset stripped Tiffany nude to further the humiliation. The relentless negative remarks about her nakedness shamed her, she felt angry at herself for allowing this treatment, she wished she were anyone else. She thought about her loved ones who weren't enduring possession and expulsion, they were probably smiling and having a good time somewhere. She was happy for them, but she so badly wanted to undo herself and join them. Her God was one of mystery and her misery would yield promises of His reward.

Those who attended the Fair left their trash and half eaten leftovers to rot at Tiffany's feet. Her spirit knew that she would get through it, but she as a person was fatigued.

'I'm a Deliverer,' a voice spoke in her mind.

Tiffany was then released from the pillory by a bolt of lightning. If she would have had a pair of scissors with her she would have plunged them somewhere or made a few openings just to release the gritty aura that was upon her. She wanted this be done, but her war was only barely midway to the conclusion.

Then, another lighting bolt struck and it formed a glass shed around Tiffany. The skies grew black and green, then a tornado ripped through the town where the perfectionists resided and destroyed every home. Without refuge, an outpouring of paint gushed from the sky and stained the albinos. Most of them took their own lives because they felt too hideous to live. The rest were caught up in a second whirlwind and thrown like ragdolls to be impaled by the limbs of trees, or landing with a lifelong disability to follow. Tiffany saw it all, still wanting to be somebody else for a few seconds. Their suffering did not excite her, instead she prayed for them to be forgiven.

Throughout the prayer, she heard the demon snarl through her lips, then a wave of negativity flooded her soul and every poor judgment she had about herself came flooding back. All the times she took things for granted, or wasn't this enough or that enough, every instance where she had a lack of confidence, they exploded like grenades within her.

"I am fearfully and wonderfully made..." she spoke aloud over and over again until she broke and let a lengthy cry out.

When she was done, she laid down on the painted splattered ground. She felt the heaviness of oppression leave her with every exhale.

"... marvelous are Thy works."

She didn't always see every angle of The Almighty's ways clearly, but she trusted Him.

She then collapsed, completely drained.

Chapter 10:
Gluttony

Tiffany couldn't recall the last time she had ate. She wasn't even sure how much time had passed since she entered the first door. She had lost a significant amount of weight, starvation was starting to settle. Her nose took in the smells from the conjoined banquet halls full of food that she was lying on the doorstep of. Her stomach seized up at the thought of sudden nourishment.

Using the arm that wasn't skinned, she crawled her way up the stairs. The doors were already open and awaiting her entry.

Every room had a table that featured a variety of her favorite foods. She was overwhelmed by the buffet, her belly begging her to begin. She was famished, the thought of the first bite was nauseating to Tiffany. Her insides felt shrunken.

Then, she felt her spirit disengage and she knew something lurked nearby. She was weak, her body could only take so much even with Divine intervention.

The initial room that she came upon was full of wings in every flavor imaginable. If she wanted dipping sauces, the supply seemed limitless for those too. She nibbled at one, then two, then she had a plate full of them. As she digested, a demonic enzyme sped up her metabolism as her body processed the sustenance. When nothing but a plate of bones was in front of her, she seen what other offers were available.

The next room was filled with pastries of every variety. Tiffany felt as if she hadn't even eaten any of the wings, but her dizziness was fading as digestion worked its course. She pondered for a second or two on what Christ felt after ending His fast, how good what was eaten must have tasted to His longing taste buds. The possibilities of pastry goodness at her fingertips felt euphoric. Each of her favorite flavors were available in assorted ways. She indulged without thinking, her soul and flesh feigning for more.

She dashed to the next room, feeling something take ahold of her and guide her there. The slices of pizza here brought to context just how many varieties there are on the market. Tiffany's top pick toppings were everywhere, they consisted of barbeque sauce, mozzarella, red onions and chicken. Her eyes were wide with desire, their color drained from her metabolic rate. The discoloration evident of the life sucking that each swallow was doing to her insides. The edible delights were laced with a string of poisons. Everything corrupting her had it all planned, right down to the order of their conquering. Demons too orchestrated steps, they often imitated their Creator. Every infliction from their kingdom was done as insult.

Tiffany engorged herself, unable to control her eagerness. The demons got high off of their use of her as a vessel for defiling. They knew she would come out victorious so they used their advantage fully while it lasted. She stuffed her mouth with pie styles she had only seen in movies, just barely breathing from her undisciplined ravaging.

She was brought to the next room without much coherence in how she came to be where she was. She was suddenly just overeating on croissants of all types. She felt full, yet still she couldn't slow down her devouring.

The poison didn't waste time in having an affect on Tiffany. Her excess was justified by her insatiable guts. She hadn't been focused on anything but overindulgence, but now she just felt unwell. She knew what food poisoning felt like, but this was worse. She swore that her intestines were full of tacks and it felt as if they were poking holes in her entrails. Her chest was ablaze with indigestion that rose up her throat and up through her nasal system.

"If they drink any deadly thing, it shall not harm them," she panted with a scorched tongue.

She then went into a coma, as the poisons seeped through her skin, leaving her in a puddle of the purged sin. It would take her body a few days to recover from the impacts of the toxins. Her spirit needed rest too, the clashes were nothing short of challenging on her as a whole.

Chapter 11:

Impure Infestation

Tiffany woke up back at her place. She had enough battling for now. She had let the main sins have their way with her soul, but she had overcome. It was on to the next trial.

The poisonous buffet had caused Tiffany's body to deplete of her stored nutrition. She didn't want to partake in anymore eating, but she needed to. No matter how many repairs or healings God provided, she was still only human after all.

The refrigerator was unplugged and empty. When she opened the cupboard, she retched. As if more taunting was necessity, her shelves were lined with nothing but cans of beanie weenies. She felt a sting of post traumatic stress disorder upon seeing the cans that carried traumatic value. Growing up, she would be forced to eat the instant slop in the dark if she complained about what was served. She shuddered, then shut the cabinets.

When the door was flush, she heard a disembodied giggle, followed by a few stifled versions. Tiffany spun around, eyes searching for the humored trespasser.

She was supposed to be home alone.

The direction of the giggling yielded nothing unordinary, but opposite of where it had come from had two blue eyes illuminating in the shadowed corner. They weren't looking at Tiffany, their stare was directed towards the corner from which the giggles had originated.

Still, nothing was there.

Tiffany was about to pray for discernment when a figure appeared. It disappeared, then reappeared beside her.

"Shhhh, no need for all that," the demon spoke with soothing syllables.

The demon wrapped an arm around Tiffany's shoulders then burst into a scarf of her great grandmother's. When it snuggly constricted her airways, she realized what the blue eyes, that were now staring directly at her, belonged to and she was made in 1903. A family heirloom. A doll wearing a white dress that had turned yellow over the decades. The same doll that was now levitating herself towards Tiffany.

"A little tighter," the doll said with the voice of the demon.

The scarf obeyed and the squeezing caused Tiffany to let out an involuntarily cough. Tiffany dropped to her knees, the doll followed to maintain eye contact.

"Would you like to see your Gram? No, that wouldn't work with someone like you would it? You know the demonic realm is the source of almost all hauntings. Coming as familiar people, deceiving, oppressing and possessing."

Tiffany retched and let out a squeal as the tightening continued. She was barely able to get an inhale through her nose.

"You're just too much fun," the doll softly and confidently smiled bearing teeth inside of her ceramic mouth.

Tiffany watched as the teeth then sharpened to points, then the doll dropped to the floor and everything stopped.

Tiffany picked up the doll and it remained lifeless. The demon may have manipulated the encounter, but there was a presence using the doll before the evil spirit intervened. Something that left off an atmosphere of sorrow. Tiffany cleared her throat, rubbing at her neck in gentle motions. When this all began, she was promised by God to be able to physically endure what the battles would do to her, while promising to keep her mental capacity tolerant also. Humans are capable of great suffering and survival, she was a testimony to the durability of a person and the supernatural capabilities of faith. Even though she knew death wouldn't come, things still made her weary. The doll showing up was unexpected, it bothered her for it to be used against her. She grit her teeth and threw the doll across the room. She landed in a position that still had her facing Tiffany with those blue eyes.

Tiffany felt the somber spirit again and fetched her Ouija. No occultist symbols were drawn this time. There was something off about the third party. It wasn't demonic. The planchette didn't move, but the doll appeared instead then she flipped over the board. The blue eyes pierced Tiffany's soul, then the doll transferred itself to her. Tiffany went rigid as she hardened to ceramic. Her imagination took over her eyesight and she saw why the sad spirit was reaching out. Only a glimpse, then the doll plopped to the ground and Tiffany's skin softened in texture.

"Free me," the doll gasped in the vocals of an exasperated man.

The blue eyes gazed at Tiffany, but it was as if the puppeteer had lost power.

No demonic trickery was afoot for awhile while Tiffany's arm grew back its covering.

It was when her skin was replaced that the trapped spirit revisited.

Tiffany was jarred awake by hands grasping her at her arm pits and knee caps. They threw her against wall vertically and then held her there.

The doll was on the bed but facing away from Tiffany. She could see the reflections of the blue eyes in her most recent paint by numbers project.

Then the painting took on the blue eyes and looked her way. More unseen fingers dug their way to her ribcage and grabbed the bones. The hands gripped her and slammed her against the wall, cracking the skeleton in her midsection in multiple places.

The paint by numbers began to streak, spelling out the words from before.

"I don't know how, or what your situation even is," Tiffany winced, her skeletal core miserable with every breath that she took.

The transparent phalanges released her broken ribcage, then a series of kitchen knives stuck in her wrists and ankles, acting like pins. The hands holding her at her knees and underarms also liberated their holds. An additional pair of knives were driven into her chest, one in each breast.

The doll was then at her right ear, whispering over and over the same phrase of needing help. When she didn't comply, she floated to the front of Tiffany and began to batter her with repetitive head butted strikes. The ceramic didn't break until the tenth hit, then a chunk fell out of the doll's forehead leaving a triangle shaped hole.

Once the doll drew blood, blue paint filled Tiffany's irises, allowing her admittance to a trench that had a spirit without an identity. It was all black as if the original owner of it had been censored from being made known to her. Copies of her great grandmother's doll were tumbling down into the furrow, all of them had only hooks for hands. The spirit in the ditch had no hands at all, just stumps, which put it at a disadvantage since climbing was the only way out. Making a climb was tough to do with shredded calves from dolls with curved prosthetics. Another figure was at the top, identity also concealed, cheering for the one below. Unfortunately for the cheerleader, the dolls were being dispensed from within it.

"The job is impossible," the doll admitted with a tone of defeat.

Blue streaks ran down Tiffany's cheeks as the vision cleared away.

"I don't know how to help," Tiffany confessed.

"While most hauntings are demonic pranks, there's some occurrences that stem from spirits trapped in *Events*, purgatory dimensions. I come from a cursed bloodline and my untimely demise caused a glitch. A reason why an *Event* occurs differs. The spirit world plays by cosmic rules, as you know. For me, I am forever stuck among the dolls and eternally separated from my best friend."

"But, what can I do?"

"Not you, but the greater one inside," the doll revealed, placing a ceramic hand to her heart.

"Call upon Him and be saved. I have nothing to do with it."

The knives were then taken out of her, causing Tiffany to fall to the bed below. The doll fell to her side, unpossessed. Tiffany cuddled it and slept.

Tiffany dreamt she was on a path meant only for her, a way to conquer her phobias. She never reached it in the dream.

When she awoke, she was en route already. Everything was the same, so she walked in the same manner as she had seen.

Chapter 12:
Sequences Of Dispelling, Part One

Tiffany's route was a dead end with a screen door in the middle of nothing. Any land beyond the door had broken pathways and couldn't be used. She couldn't see beyond the entryway, whatever was behind it was hidden. When she opened the door, there was nothing but a manhole. The spacing looked tight, she knew that fear would be making the trip with her.

"God keep me sane," she whispered as she entered the hole head first.

"He will be taking a backseat, dear. You're mine now," the demon that had interfered before suavely interjected.

Tiffany closed her eyelids, it was pitch black anyways but for some reason closing her eyes kept her faith and thoughts aligned.

She was in a tunnel of rock just big enough to enable her to army crawl.

"Make it count," she snarled to the one creeping into her soul.

Her eyes stayed closed, but her hands were no longer hers. They quit moving forward along with the rest of her.

Then her hands peeled something plastic off of the nearby rocks. Her spirit snarled as it then wrapped it around her face. Tiffany's heart sped as the demon lurched her into the winding, constricted tunnel. The demon was excited and it caused Tiffany's expression under the unwanted mask to have a smile.

Then, she hit a wall of rocks and couldn't go any further.

The possession ended, leaving her without spiritual assistance. Her heart played out of beat as if a practicing drummer, her lungs locked up as she did her best to breathe. Her limbs were all too tightly confined for her to remove her crude veil, the tunnel had narrowed. Then she tried to move backwards and could not. She was buried under rock, underground and nobody knew. She tried to think a prayer, but her brain wasn't being supplied enough oxygen to allow thought processes. She didn't want to pass out, but her mortal well being depended on it.

Tiffany came to still inside a coffin of rock, but the plastic wasn't wrapped around her skull any longer. She felt her heart in palpitations, her breathing system sputtered as it struggled to not collapse.

Once she was breathing, the fear overcame her again and allowed her to creep ahead in the engulfing blackness. Her own hands again put on the unwanted mask and she got suspended in the unconscious darkness, vulnerable to anything that the demon found entertaining.

He isn't keeping you alive, I am.

She was one with the spirit of fear.

Your panicky stench is like pheromones, Tiffany.

Her lungs buckled and heaved in her chest cavity, her throat strangled by vines of anxiety.

Even he can't save you now.

Tiffany was livid at the blasphemy, her soul came in to agreement that Tiffany's body wouldn't be able to withstand the perpetual asphyxia.

You just might die down here.

Milliseconds before she would be sent in a mind melting seizure, she came up out of the rocky pit.

Fear withdrew its influence.

Tiffany tore the plastic away and clutched herself. Every time that she exhaled, she screamed.

She was on the ground shrieking for hours.

Once Tiffany stood, strands of doll hair coiled around her throat and pulled her back down. The blue eyes of the ceramic heirloom led her down another tunnel, this one was sand. The eye contact stole Tiffany's air, she would do this grainy tunnel holding her breath. She heard the doll breathing as it pulled her along the sandy subterranean passage.

The sands packed Tiffany's mouth as the fear settled in again and forced her to intake.

I've always ran my tongue up and down your soul when you were scared. Tasty Tiff, I call you among my pals.

Tiffany's body then stiffened as she kept going against the grain. Her eyes never leaving the lifeless stare of her great grandmother's doll.

After a miles and miles of being dragged, the doll's hair unwrapped from around her neck and broke eye contact.

Tiffany had no usage of her limbs at first, but eventually she found her bearings.

She would hack up sand periodically for a long time after.

Chapter 13:
Sequences Of Dispelling, Part Two

Tiffany came up out of the second tunnel and found a well there. Nothing else, therefore only one way to go once again. The backdrop was all nothingness, a shore of the outer darkness.

"The worst is over, Tiff. Now, you'll see wonders that many fear only in their nightmares. They exist. I'll show you."

The demon then handed Tiffany scuba gear that she dressed in. Once she had it on and the oxygen mask placed, fear again overran her soul.

I'll be your guide, Tiffany. Today, we'll be exploring the parts of the ocean that no submarine can visit.

Oh and we take another tunnel, fun, huh?

The chuckling demon that was invading her had a calm demeanor and she understood why fearful moments were so sly. The slightest discomfort could be an arsenal at the disposal of this vile being.

Tiffany was in a rotation of whirlpools, acting as a thread to a needle in their epicenters. Each eye she entered was a portal to the bottom. As the currents weakened, Tiffany saw through the eyes of fear. The demon and her were looking at an oversized alligator that had the flesh and fins of a shark, the snout of the creature was the shape of a hammerhead.

The sea experiments of your beloved.

Tiffany swam through another underwater black hole, and came out to a school of dolphins with human skin that were munching on the carcass of a whale made of coral.

The next wonders were a few hippopotamus that were comprised of seaweed that was bound together by fish scales.

He in heaven sure is creative, aren't we glad to be enjoying this moment together?

Up next, there were clams that had jellyfish tentacles with enlarged nematocysts on them. They were fighting against a barrage of seahorses with crab arms and pincers that considered them a delicacy.

The rotating waters were speeding up, thrashing Tiffany and her possessor in a maelstrom. The swirling gave her seasickness and she threw up.

The vortex spit her out in front of a prehistoric turtle whose dermis was sea shells. She was the size equivalent to the amphibian's eyeball. It sucked her in its mouth, then spat her out.

Tiffany glided through the water like a torpedo, passing an octopus with the bristles and markings of a black widow spider.

She hurled past a cave that was having a scientific contest between nautical Martians. The theme was human skeletons, dozens of entries were present.

Tiffany was then brought to a wrecked ship, the crew were strewn about the deck in ragged pieces. She squirmed her way to a treasure chest, then it opened up and out floated a decrepit clone of her great grandmother's doll. It snatched her scuba diving gear from her which meant Tiffany had to once more test the limits of her pulmonary function.

Tiffany ascended towards the surface, a school of pufferfish with bat wings nipped at her bare feet with their razor sharp piranha cusps.

When she reached the top, there weren't waves nor sky nor oxygen, there was sleeping demons that held glass shards in their anatomies. She launched her fists against them, but they didn't respond. Bubbles escaped from her mouth as the pufferfish were closing in on her ankles.

You've been a most pleasant host, but your faith precedes you.

Tiffany drowned in salty aqua as she praised God for delivering her back to a sound mind. The spirit of fear was swallowed up by a downdraft and dispelled back to the oceanic depths.

Tiffany was rescued by a fellow named Colvin who sported a mouth of gold. He pulled her from the waters and made sure she didn't choke her upheavals.

Tiffany beat her fears, but it was time for her to rest. Her spirit too desired a pause.

She gave thanks before falling asleep in her bed with her great grandmother's doll, it was her honor to quarrel on behalf of her God. She slept soundly.

Chapter 14:
Tiffany Gets Her Braces

Tiffany's thirteenth dealing was a simpler exorcism, but it was after she drove away her soul infections that she had a different encounter. Just as her chest was heaving less, a wind blew through her house that carried a voice with it.

"You've been disrupting the realms. Time is already short, your work here is only quickening the end's pace," the breeze harshly spoke, each word leaving behind cuts across Tiffany's anatomy.

When Tiffany saw whom was speaking to her, she almost doubted her sanity. Before her stood a thing with the torso of a man, his forearms were metal rods, while his hands were large anvils. She would have thought this all symptoms of a night terror had she not witnessed the fruits of other existing dimensions numerous times before this. Her body was often a battleground between realms. Scars were left, but she was always provided with a way to press on and not see defeat. She opened her mouth to rebuke her visitor, but an anvil swung and broke her jaw.

"You may understand your demons, but there's entities much more powerful than them. Save your denunciation for the ones deserving. Your battles are going to escalate now that I have shown myself."

Tiffany found it interesting that he didn't reference the strange knobs atop his shoulders as a face, there was no head, only what she assumed were a pair of eyes. The knobs were at the end of a pair of inverted hooks that were plastic. With no lower extremities below the torso, Tiffany charged the thing and tackled him into an armoire. Both Tiffany and the thing landed violently against the antique dresser. The anvils' weight made the thing slow, Tiffany took the advantage to attack him with a fury of kicks and punches. Grunts upon intense gusts came from the thing as the blows struck him. He struggled to stand as Tiffany beat him with all that was within her. Bruises appeared on the parts of the thing that were flesh, then Tiffany curved her fingers to resemble claws and began to tear away chunks of his skin. As she was digging away at his left shoulder rotator, he managed to fling her away. She landed hard, then an anvil crushed her right femur. She cried out, but an air current swept down her throat and lined it with incisions. There were syllables and phrases riding the inhaled draft.

"There's no seconds for me to waste on you. I must find the one that seeks to hemmor age and get the individual to the altar before my anvils can rust. If they become rusty, it seals my damnation. The decay of metal is a sign of the eternally condemned. It is my mission to ensure that the altar is reached and a hemmor age occur. Without that separation of the final human's body and spirit, flesh will live beyond the realm it was intended to remain in, causing unimaginable consequences in the realms of the eternal."

When the voice quit talking, the thing turned on his elongated arms and walked away using his anvils to act as his feet. He sweated droplets of blood that trailed behind him, as he left Tiffany to tend to her split jawline.

Tiffany was blessed enough to keep all of her teeth in the break, but braces would be necessary to keep them secured.

Chapter 15:
Visceral Visitation

Candles and a board with words sat in front of Tiffany again. Led by her spirit, she began to use the planchette to spell out names that she couldn't audibly pronounce. She dismissed each arrival, until she spelled out a name that made the floors of her house creak. The front door rocked off the hinges, then Tiffany felt a shift in her eyeballs and everything she saw changed. The world around her was abruptly alive, surreal and nothing but shadows, in the midst of the gloom stood a fallen angel that towered over her small frame. She had built some solid muscle up since weakening the seven primary demons and conquering her fears, but this behemoth made the most massive lifters look frail. She had evoked many times before this, but those were demons and typically easily expelled. She gulped roughly, her new vision contained within the spiritual realm. She turned towards the mirror and looked in her alive eyes, but this time saw a burning ring of light in the center of the darkness. The muscular entity lunged at her and wrapped enlarged phalanges around her throat to squeeze her oxygen supply out. Her lungs pushed out, the fallen one pushed in. She felt her heart race as the bulky entity fit itself in the confines of her, as impossible as it all seemed. Her flesh seized up, breaking open with incisions as her epidermis attempted to expand to allow the intruder to settle. Blood started to collect below her as she began to levitate, her expression turning purplish from the internal strangulation. Her wrists and ankles shifted to break in every place possible. Her bone shards stuck out in awkward positions, all dangling as if detached.

As she fought an instant asthma attack, her eyes saw a second angel come to her aid. This one wasn't humanly in appearance, it was a four winged creature with feathers of rusted blades that blinked in a specific sequence, in the center mass of the being was an eye that didn't blink. The wings spun and sliced up the enemy, drenching the shadowy area with angelic gore. Demons that were tiny compared to the fallen angel showed up and fought against the winged eyeball. They tore at the razors that made up the quad wingspan, trying to dislodge the dicing mechanisms. They looked almost extraterrestrial in appearance, not anything like the movies she enjoyed showed. They were ugly and deformed, nothing like either angel. She had only felt them previously, but now she could see them tangibly. Some were effeminate, others were studious. All hid well in the black, only illuminated by the fire in Tiffany's eyes. They pricked their fingers in her lungs and stole pockets of her element, while she gasped out a memorized Psalm. The recital drove away the demons, but the angels were still battling it out and saturating everything in their blood. Both bled, neither backed down.

Tiffany scrambled for her Bible, flipping it open to lash out the words against the wicked one. Turning the pages was a daunting task with splintered wrists, but she pushed through it. The pages tore and clung to her as she read aloud.

She could feel something swirling in her lungs, crawling or swimming, trying to eradicate their supply. She dropped to her knees, clenching her fists, bleeding from the cuts caused by her manicured nails. The drips fell in the red puddles that gathered in the grooves of the carving of the pentagram that she held these sessions in. She began to feel doubt creep in, making her wonder if another battle would ensue. Had she met her match? All things were claimed possible, she staked her confidence in the promise. The pessimistic idea of her failing was cast aside by the sudden decapitation of the fallen angel. One of the four wings had slashed it off in a rapid succession of edges.

It was over.

Tiffany tried to catch her breath, her eyelids forced shut. The room looked untouched to her natural eye, the physical realm the only one showing now. Had she not seen it occur, she would not have known that a vicious beheading just went down. She unburied her nails from her palms, her clothes were tattered, proving that the demons had been more aggressive than she had realized in her struggle.

Chapter 16:
Combatting A Liar

A sudden frigid temperature overtook her bedroom, whoever was coming to see what all the commotion was about was powerful. Or at least wanted her to think that way, she felt a phoniness about the coming enemy.

The glass slid from all of her windows and fell to the floor without breaking. In the reflections, she saw a being made of a million pink tongues that wriggled like a colony of maggots. The father of all liars was in each reflection, then the mirror in the room split into several splintered pieces but remained in tact. The middle piece fell out, then Lucifer stepped out and stood before Tiffany. In a peripheral, he might look hairy Tiffany noted, but the case was not so, he was built like a puny man with living slivers of boils. His skin looked slimy from the decades of deceit that layered his dishonest spirit. The glass in the mirror then burst to fragments causing the walls to seep serpents that talked in human languages and only spoke words of condemnation. They ridiculed Tiffany with every mistake or hurtful insult possible. Then, Lucifer snapped his fingers and it all evaporated.

Tiffany stood alone, none of the broken shards reflecting anything. Her intuition felt something amiss, then she felt a slimy hand crawl up her spine and poke through the back of her neck to grab a handful of her brunette hair strands. Her head was pulled back, then a second hand forced her mouth open to receive the slithering caterpillar of blood clots that was inching overtop of her. She tried to gurgle a prayer, but the goopy worm slid down her opening before she could manage a rebuke. The clots burst apart and began to consume her soul, giving her unto the liar for control. Her ankles and wrists violently snapped back into place.

Tiffany hunched over in a manner that should have broke her spinal cord, yet she was able to twist unnaturally. Her ears blared with verbal abuse based on the past. She could hear whispers from somewhere unspecified that tried to convince her that this was all acceptable and her new constant. If her mouth would confess this reality as true, she would lose. The balance between the spiritual and physical would merge and alter everything that ever existed on Earth.

Redemption was the key, her spirit discerned that the angel of blades was the one that had put it in Lucifer's thoughts to rebel against God, as well as tempting The Watcher angels with lust for the women of Earth. Suggestions that were meant to test faith, only reaped destruction and falls. The wings of the seraphim corroded over time, tainted by the corruptions spawned from his temptations. The deterioration went on until the death and resurrection of God's begotten.

Tiffany scoffed at the grand deceiver before her, but the bones in her limbs all started to pop in various places as spurs broke out like hives. Foam poured from Tiffany's mouth as she continued to contort and coil. Lies and condemning speech lashed out from nowhere, orbiting Tiffany's possessed soul that absorbed the decay into her subconscious. The lies saturated her soul and she had never felt more used. With her arms and legs still coiled like corkscrews, she began to use her teeth to snap her nails from her hands and feet. Her eyes blackened, vigorous by her revisited traumas and the energy that her despair was feeding to Lucifer and his demons. When she started to make attempts to open up her radial arteries via her braces, her eyes lit up with a white fire and out from the mirror stepped a refined version of the angel with the eye in the center that she had previously encountered. He had blades still, but they weren't rusty like before, they were precious metals that looked polished. The centered eye was narrowed, burning with the ring of light Tiffany previously saw in her own. The wings still blinked as if they were the angel's eyelids. The iris remained ablaze, but the pupil of the eye dilated and contracted as he spoke in an angelic tongue that sounded timeless. Lucifer assaulted the winged eyeball, his pink tongues vomiting out acid that attempted to corrode the feathery edges and turn them back to rust. The bone spurs sprouted, giving birth to tongues that protruded up and through Tiffany's flesh. The angel's eye softened, but then glared again. He would end what he had begun, even if it meant Tiffany would be maimed or butchered in the process.

In awkward motions, Tiffany leaped up the wall to avoid being struck and was able to navigate her mangled limbs as if it were natural. The protruding tongues flailed against her skin and Tiffany could taste their putrid matter in her own mouth. She sat in the corner with her back to the angel, but her head spun fully, ready for a backflip pounce. Instead of jumping to strike, she began to cough out blood clots that floated out to surround the angel of blades. They burst upon him and turned parts of him rusty once more. Tiffany watched it all like she were viewing a first person film, out of her control despite her being the main character. The wingspan reached the opposing walls, then the angel swiped aggressively at Tiffany, severing many of the tongues, while removing layers of skin from Tiffany's arms and legs. Her body knew the pain but disassociated from it. She prayed in her head, her vocal cords too coated with a rusted clot to allow verbalizing. Her body thrashed in the corner, her blood running down the walls like artwork. The partial tongues shriveled up and died, leaving only holes across Tiffany's limbs. The angel made an X motion with his wings, then left Tiffany an amputee. Red gushed from her amputations, then the possession ended and Lucifer left Tiffany's soul. She dropped down hard, breaking her spinal column in multiple places, then she blacked out.

Chapter 17:
Sacrifice And Restoration

Tiffany's removed limbs sat on the floor, covered in holes where a liar once mastered her soul, disintegrating from the acidic properties of the severed tongues. Her voice was hoarse, but she lifted her chin and looked past the four wings with her splashed blood decorating them, then yelled incoherently from her spirit so that only her Lord could comprehend. When she was done, the eye of the angel stared at her dying form and decided it was time for his selfless act.

"May The Almighty always know that I am pitifully sorry for my suggestion. It was not my place to test faith, it is only His," the angel spoke in simple English, then he turned to rust and froze forever.

The prototype of those angels crafted in the image of the Holy Ghost sat still, a statue to serve as a reminder of a tale of rebellion and redemption. Tiffany grew back her removed parts, keeping the scars to serve as tattoos to inspire her constant progression no matter the odds against her.

Mourning Beyond

The doors were latched, then guns were drawn by the robbers wearing masquerade masks that covered their entire faces. One of them stepped to the counter, then pointed a barrel directly at the clerk. The staff was petrified with shock, what they had assumed was a prank had just taken a serious turn. Ballroom wearing costumers had seemed innocent initially, but then the weapons appeared.

"We've been watching. The trucks, the massiveness of this place, it is clear you store things here of incredible value."

"Our cargo is very precious, yes."

"We intend to leave with it today, all of it."

The clerk chuckled, then excused himself for the abrupt chuckles. The masked bandit then fired a bullet through the clerk's forehead. Outbursts by the other employees were quickly subdued with guns being put against heads.

"Listen up, there's two options here today. One, you give us what we came for. Two, everybody employed here today retires early as a result of insubordination."

"Shouldn't fire gunshots," one of the clerks warned.

"Nobody tells me," the woman snarled through her fancy covering, pressing the gun's barrel to the bridge of the clerk's nose.

She then stepped around the clerk, putting the tip of the firearm to the back of his balding cranium.

"Now, let's get moving towards the vaults before my hand ends up in more gun powder."

Twig was quiet as he went to his dad's home for visitation. He was glad to be there, but not when his dad's girlfriend's daughter was over. She was kind enough around others, but when it was just her and Twig, she liked to trigger his claustrophobia. She would giggle maniacally as he wept in fear trapped under the blanket. Sometimes she would remove the soft covering of terror to taste his tears. Once they were licked up, Twig was again trapped under suffocating fibers.

"Open it, one try," the woman in charge warned.

The vault door was vast. If money or jewels were on the opposite side, then there had to be mountains of it.

A clicking sound made a smirk appear behind the bandit's mask.

"Promise me that you won't shoot," the balding clerk negotiated.

Silence came from behind the masquerade mask, nothing else. The barrel was pressed hard to his temple to get the point across.

"I didn't mean me, I meant the precious cargo," the clerk added, then he spun the spokes of the handle and opened the vault door.

It creaked open, then an enormous croaking sound filled the quietness. The green eyes behind the exquisite mask of the robber went wide. Then, she put the barrel of the gun to the back of the clerk's neck.

"Where's the treasures?"

The clerk chuckled in mockery, then the trigger finger of the bandit squeezed and a single shot ceased his employment.

Twig never spoke of the abuse, but the trappings traumatized him. He began to develop anxieties that he didn't previously have. Even with the traumatic experiences with blankets, Twig couldn't sleep uncovered, though he never pulled them up over his own chin, ever.

Three gunmen with elegant face coverings and expensive suits jogged to the back. Their automatic weapons ready for massacre.

"Relax, boys. Go and fetch another guide, mine expired."

The duo did as they were told, bringing back a guy with a moustache that curled upwards.

"What is this place? Dishonesty makes things messy," the leading lady barked, nodding towards the other dead clerk.

"A bank..."

"No. Not just a bank. We came for riches, rarities, but so far I've only seen a monster!"

"This bank is where we store Miscreations."

The tip of the gun was pushed against the man's cleft. The woman felt the groove beneath the concealing hair above his upper lip.

"Unlock them all. Every door."

The clerk did as he was told, then he was executed. She then turned to her partners.

"Destroy every specimen you find."

The next week came around, Twig found himself alone with his tormentor once again. She had gotten a bigger blanket, heavier, less breathable. Heather immediately threw it over his head and held the ends to keep him underneath, just as she always did. Twig panicked, his vision seeing only darkness and his breathing organs allotted minimum use.

Hours passed with Twig bawling, not once was the blanket removed. Deciding he had enough of her sadism, he tried to find an edge to slip through. He maneuvered himself for a long time, not finding a blanket opening nor the edge of the bed.

After his breathing had become gasps of desperation, he found a corner of the blanket that was open. He assumed that the girl had turned a light on but was surprised to see that he was outside.

It was a place unlike any he had ever seen. The sky was pink and orange, the air warm and cheerful. There was a shuffle to his left, then a group of people surrounded Twig.

"Where's your smile?"

Twig felt confused, his cranium tilting like an intrigued dog. He didn't ask what they meant, because it dawned on him that they had permanent grins, wide and toothy. Two of them had zippers that ran up one side of their mouths, across the bottom of their noses, and ended on the opposite side of their lips. The other three had a single button on either side of their mouth where their dimples should have been. The one thing they all had in common were their matching smiles. Their other features varied.

"I sm-smile a lot-t," Twig stammered, suddenly feeling self conscious.

"But not always?"

Twig felt singled out for his ability to frown.

"Where I come from... people don't always smile, it doesn't mean they're unhappy."

"Unhappiness doesn't exist here. It never has. Our elders once knew words such a pain, loss, death. Not us, and only one elder still lives."

"All hail Queen Szejna," all the ones with indefinite smiles cheered in unison.

"A land of only happiness? But, how?"

"Only Queen Szejna is permitted to speak of things unhappy. Ask her why and she might tell."

"Can you take me to her?"

Everyone but Twig was smiling, so he joined in. Then, the group started towards where Queen Szejna was. Their trek led them across lavender sands with yellow pebbles.

Automatic weapons fired upon the clownfish colored frog as it leaped out of an in-ground pool. The frog's lengthy tongue lashed out at the gunmen like a whip, the end of it the metasoma of a scorpion. It stung one of them and he fell, his gun still unloading bullets.

The other exquisitely dressed assailants then blew the Miscreation apart, leaving bits of it on land, and pieces of it floating in the waters meant for wading. As the venomous frog was dying, the venom it had injected brought forth the painful conclusion of another life.

Yellow pebbles slipped between Twig's toes as he stood in front of Queen Szejna. He buried his feet in the pink sands as he felt her blue eyes pierce his soul.

"You're in the wrong dimension," she studied aloud.

She had eyebrows drawn on, freckles sat scattered across her nose and cheeks. She too wore a smile, but it was kept on with an elastic band that went around her head. Her hair was brown and curly.

"Well, if this dimension is wrong for me. Where am I, and where do I belong? I'm Twig by the way."

Queen Szejna kept her smiling gaze.

"You've crossed a threshold somehow. This is a land between the halves of the Earths. Tucked away from their societies of violence and sorrow. You will find no tolerance of any unhappiness here. I am Queen Szejna, founder of this colony."

"Are all the others your children?"

"No. My children all are grown. Elizabeth is a Librarian, and Alexandria is a Revolutionist. They are powerful, pivotal women. They remain where you originate from. I stay here. We communicate regularly though."

"Do you miss seeing them?"

"Not as much as I miss my Jasper. He was a special boy."

"Was that your husband?"

"No. He was the last pet that I ever had."

With that, the conversation concluded and Twig woke up back in the room of his dad's apartment. He was still covered up, but Heather was nowhere around.

In the lobby, gun barrels pointed at the remaining clerk, and at the customer that was inside at the time of the takeover. The multiple firings of gunshots had everyone wondering what was happening in the back of the building.

Every movement of the robbers was choreographed, their steps almost rhythmic as if they were not robbing a bank but performing a dance routine during a fancy Ball. They were precise, structured and bloodthirsty.

The next vault, contained a parliament of owls with scales. In between the plates of each scale were porcupine quills. When they turned their necks around, the thin razors would launch in every direction. One of the slender spikes took out both eyes of one of the gunmen. A mixture of blood and eye juice spilled from the wound. The owls swooped down and began to peck apart the man's Ballroom appropriate mask.

The other gunman was dealing with a few hostile hooters too when suddenly a rapid succession of bullets eliminated the struggle on both sides.

The woman in charge then stood over the lifeless corpses of her henchmen and kicked holes in them with her heels, it was the only time that she broke her strides of choreography.

Twig was bummed when he went to his dad's and Heather was not there. He was eager to try to get back to the happy place. Careful not to be raising suspicion by asking about her whereabouts, he spent the weekend watching a cartoon about a grasshopper with wooden wagon wheel legs that solved inter-dimensional mysteries. He wondered if he would do the same with Queen Szejna and her smiling bunch.

With considered steps, the woman leading the robbery danced her way to the next vault, only after placing her deceased partners in a proper pose that matched their fancy attire. She armed herself with the automatic weapons from her colleagues and threw the door open. Several gunshots rang out from the front of the bank, so she closed the door without peering inside.

She trotted merrily to the front and was confronted by a brunette wearing the face covering of her now dead assailant. The two mask wearers stared at each other as if locked in a duel, barrels unwavering in their hands.

"Always has to be a hero," the robber spat with disgust.

"Let me make my withdrawal and I'll be on my way."

"The assets in this place deserve extermination. They're experiments."

"Let us go. He was only here temporarily, I came today to get him out."

"Picked the wrong day, eh? Well, let's go see this precious pet...

You're leading the way."

One gun lowered, while the other stayed pointed at the back of the brunette's skull. Her curly hair shined under the burning fluorescents overhead. The woman running the operation thought it would be a pity make it matted with gooey DNA. She waited until the door was opened before firing a bullet through the customer's cranium. She then looked in at the long legs of the black cat and caught a glimpse of white toes on his back, left foot. It pounced on her, then pinned her to the floor. His tail then raised high, a barbed stinger sat at the end of it. The attacks were swift, one to the abdomen, three in the neck, then two to the skull. The venomous spikes penetrated with ease. Snotty, pitiful yelling was abruptly replaced by gurgled convulsions as the leading woman lost her position. Before she died, she managed to get a grenade loose from the inside of her corset. She pulled the pin and everything within the vast deposit box erupted in fire and gore. The cat was blown in half, only the foot with the white toes and half of the cat's face was not left mangled up or ragged. He had lived through the explosion, but the injuries were severe.

The woman in the hallway sobbed beneath the mask that she was wearing, her curls sticky and caked in vital fluid. Her heavy crying made the decorative design of the mask she wore seem sinister. It was crafted to bring delight, but the harrowing sounds coming from her womb could only be delightful to a sadist. With her hands placed against the eye holes of the mask, the tears flowed through the cracks of her fingers, down her hands and moistened the generous amount of freckles covering her forearms. The cat nudged her, purring to let her know that he was going to make it, but she knew that he would have to recover someplace apart from any Earth. A place where the Miscreations went to retreat and revive. The beings that dwelled there among the Miscreations were almost human, except that they didn't have natural expressions or emotions. Her husband had told her about it before his sudden disappearance. The cat peeled off her mask, then licked her face. He had to go soon and where he had to be was a no trespassing zone for those not Miscreated.

Twig didn't like the apartment too much, it had bugs crawling in the shadows within the cabinets. He retreated to the bedroom, another weekend not at mom's. He heard the voice of his antagonist, who then came into the room and shut the door behind her.

"We're trying something fresh this time, Twig," Heather chuckled as she revealed an oversized plastic bag.

"This is too far..."

"Quiet down. It is a short game called 'ten seconds of trauma'. Once you go, I will."

Before Twig could consent, his head was covered and his eyes rolled back to somewhere else.

The lids of the customer's eyes revealed a brilliant blue when they were open. She went to her vehicle, then returned inside the bank with a vial. She then collected the spilt blood of her special cat. She hadn't used the Veterinary equipment for years, but she had held on to all of her college year stuff, thankfully. Once the vial was full, she left the bank after opening up the vaults to let the others loose.

Twig woke up in a dark reflection of the happy land. The sands and sky were black, even the moon was a deep crimson. Aboriginables, nemeses of the Miscreations, lurked here. They were the living metals of the Earth, pieced together to be executioners.

"We know one with skin is here," one of them taunted.

Twig sprinted, unable to see anything but black and red.

"Been a long while since we had a human trophy to slaughter. Come out, Twig. To dice is my vice, but I'd settle for slicing or stabbing."

Twig stepped on something extremely sharp, as metal figures that intended to make him suffer surrounded his frail body.

Then, the bag was removed and Twig awoke wheezing while Heather uncontrollably laughed. The fear in his eyes had lit the girl up with giddiness.

The collected samples of the cat served dual purposes. One, it could allow her passage to where the Miscreations hid. Two, there was rumor of a girl that sometimes crossed the lands of the Miscreations that knew someone that claimed to be able to repair the mismatched creations and was working on a variety of innovative ideas involving them. She felt it somewhat exploiting to ask the stranger for assistance, but she wanted to help her friend. She needed to aid his healing, it was in her nature to do so.

She pricked each of her fingers, then dipped them in the vial of DNA. She felt the foreign sequences travel her bloodstream, then a pathway uncovered itself before her feet. Overlaying the green grass was lavender sands with yellow pebbles sprinkled about. She took the new walkway without a shred of hesitation. She had to get to her Jasper.

The secret path ended at an extravagant gate. A blind gatekeeper stood at the entrance, sniffing. The blood from the cat overpowered her humanly smell, allowing the trespasser access.

She had kept a hold of the mask that she took from the bank robber she had killed, she slipped it on to try to blend in.

There were humanoid types here, but they had no mouths nor natural eyebrows, making their appearances expressionless. Their race were called Modifiers due to their skills in body modification. Some had implants in odd places, others had forked tongues or a variety of horns and ridges. None of it was costume, they had all adapted themselves to look as they did. Hours of dedication, pure devotion in action.

It didn't take long for the masked intruder to be outed, Szejna was interrogated immediately by a Modifier with crescent shaped moon chunks of epidermis missing, from head to toe.

"How did you get here?"

"I'm looking for a black cat that was wounded. His back, left foot has white toes."

"Humans aren't permitted to be here. You are a species that thrives on emotions."

"I only wish to find some happiness in knowing he is alright. Please."

"On one condition."

"Name it."

"You teach us about happy."

Szejna told them about adopting her eldest daughter, and birthing her youngest, and what joyous occasions they were. About her husband the writer, who had went missing. When her expression turned from uplifted to worried, some of the Modifiers demanded she omit the unhappy parts. They knew pain existed outside of their realm, the hurt Miscreations that sought refuge in their land were all they needed to see to know to steer clear of any other civilizations. Szejna taught them games, painting, rock collecting, poetry and all the things on the second Earth that had brought her happiness.

Twig didn't remember a blanket being put over him, but it must have happened because he was crawling endlessly under one. He was hopeful to go to the place with the funny looking folk.

"Almost a year it has been since that day at the bank. You all know what it means to feel joy, you have modified yourselves to always appear happy, so I am asking as your newly appointed Queen to be taken to my Jasper."

"We can show the way, but it is restricted to us."

"I understand. Take me."

The Modifiers led Queen Szejna to an orange road that had the signature of Provector Evans at the start, signed when it was freshly paved. Seeing his name made Szejna's smile she always wore fade underneath the one that never did. She had met him during her college days, and it is through him that she obtained Jasper, but she found his Zoo, and the reasons for the existence of it, painted Provector in a gray light. He didn't mistreat the Miscreations, but his purpose seemed selfish to her. His tragic murder still wasn't something she had ever hoped she would have to watch, but she had seen it happen during a broadcast of the footage. Seeing his name seemed like a sign. No matter the end result, her mission was necessary.

"Rest in peace, Pro," she whispered as she stepped over his name and continued her newfound journey.

"Hey, Twig. Good to see you again," a boy with his bones showing in various spots welcomed.

"Yeah, we wasn't sure that we would get to see you again," a girl with matching bones showing added.

They were twins, modified so that their knees, elbows, cheeks, toes and phalanges were all without skin or muscle. Their smiles were attached to their exposed cheekbones via sewing thread.

"I'm glad to be back. What's been happening? All good?"

"The Queen went on the orange road that only those with Miscreated blood travel. Otherwise, we are happy."

The three all smiled at one another, only one dissipated slowly.

"I've never seen a Miscreation."

"Your species isn't supposed to. You likely never will, unless you can stay here for longer periods."

"I'll try. I only know one way and it isn't pleasant and not usually brought on by choice."

"Well, if you want to see one then stick around sometime, Twig."

Before he could agree verbally, Twig was woken up from chest compressions by Heather.

Queen Szejna looked small in comparison to the wideness of the path that she was on. Her black and white sneakers made no noise as they stepped. There was nothing for miles that she could see, but plenty of mixed breed creatures witnessed her go by. The blood of her cat only allotted her ingress to the land, the ones that chose to remain invisible weren't able to be seen by Queen Szejna. The closer she got to Jasper, the warmer her body temperature felt. By time she reached her beloved cat, she was sweating. He looked healed, regenerated even. He tackled her with his front paws, crushing her boobs as he took her to the ground and purred. She suddenly realized that she could hear Jasper's thoughts, and the ability was going both ways.

'Szejna, so wonderful to reunite with you!'

'I've been so worrisome over you, Jasper.'

'It was a dreary process of healing. Someone helped me, she rides a dinosaur with leprosy. Unfortunately, I now carry the disease. Though I am unaffected, I cannot return with you ever again.'

'I can't stay here. You know this. I'll visit when I can.'

'I'd love that. We share blood and therefore you can never be a leper. If you see her, the one who rides the dinosaur, you won't catch it. Try to find her. She told me that she has a gift for you.'

'I'll see that I visit often, maybe I can catch her passing through. I miss you, but I'll be back. I love you, Jasper, my special boy with the foot of white toes.'

'I love you too, Queen Szejna.'

Twig knew exactly where in his throat he would need to put pressure on to pass himself out, Heather had done it enough times for him to grow in expertise. The blanket trappings had led to more serious ways of her inducing his panic. Her tactics were becoming increasingly dangerous.

He tested the belt, then leaned inwards to cut off his oxygen. He thought about seeing a Miscreation and a giant smile engulfed his face, then he blacked out.

"Queen Szejna, we found Twig. He looks unhappy."

The Queen leapt up and rushed to see what the commotion was about. When she saw his condition, she knew that she had another lesson to teach The Modifiers. One that centered around death and loss, exposing their species to the unhappiness that she had thought she had left behind. She would have to inform them of her own mortality too, one day she would have deflated lungs like Twig, it was the curse of being human. It was obvious to her that Twig had been strangled. She left that detail out and told them about a place called Heaven.

"Twig's spirit lives on then, how wonderful. You're an exceptional person, Queen Szejna. We have learned so much from you," a girl with ridged implants, and under the dermis welts, praised.

"Everything and everyone casts a shadow elsewhere. I'm sure that skinny boy is in Heaven smiling, radiating happiness. Waiting for my arrival," Queen Szejna sniffled through her smiling mask.

Everyone attending his burial was all smiles.

After burying Twig, Queen Szejna got word that Ruthie Ann was coming through. Queen Szejna thought the girl was as lovely as the ocean melody that escaped from the mouth of the Lepersaur. Just before they left, Ruthie handed Szejna an all black kitten that fit in the palm of her hand. The black, right foot had white toes on it.

"Her name is Ghastlie, she is a miniature clone of your pet. Sometimes they are mirror images when they are cloned, but I doubt you'll mind much. I'm a good person to know," Ruthie winked, then she got on the back of her dinosaur and returned to her adventures.

Queen Szejna felt the cat purr in her hand and was filled with bliss. She never again stopped smiling.

Nowan's Atonement

I watched as two of my first fans gasped for air that wouldn't come. The quality was low, had we been on Earth one, their blood would have went silver. This was no act of bloodsport, nor am I a sadist. I am simply a storyteller that will be seen one way or another. I have created, I was willing to destroy.

Corrina and Deanna were stuck in the same predicament as one another. A maze of torn out pages was their surroundings, my words jumbled and mixed up for them to sort. No page had a number, a certain way to be sure they were reading. They were given pills to suppress their appetite and bodily excretions. It was just them and my stories. Read or perish was the game's name. I wanted them to survive, but I also wanted them challenged. To do so, they were administered a dose of experimental powder meant to inhibit short term memory. They were having a Hellish time. Frustrated and disoriented, they trudged through the slender caverns of dangling pages, over a thousand of them were suspended and needing to be carefully chosen. The participants were the fans that I still needed some reviews from, that would be their task after they accomplished the book building maze.

The life of Susan rested on their goals being met. She was laid out on a table fighting for her life due to an infection. The cure was in the books that the duo I was overseeing were struggling with. If they reached Parable Terminus, the last story in that one would let them know of Susan's fate, as well as their own.

For now, we were all on a secluded island that didn't exist before I wrote it to be. I always knew I was meant to write, but a life changing situation let me know how much power I wield with my imagination. Like so few before me, there were worlds that were out there across an expanse of dimensions, each a trickle of proof that some writers have the gift of creation. I, however, was writing things that would come to fruition in my own realm. Likely, the very one that anybody that reads this is in. The one with that animated bunny that wants to know, "what's up, Doc?", originated in. I call it Earth two, but none of this is too relevant to this tale.

These two had written some of my absolute favorite reviews, so I was eager for them to finish my series, even though I knew the likelihood wasn't in their favor. They couldn't stop their movements because I was in complete control of everything as I typed their every move and made them read. They looked so tired, but they pressed on as they I wrote them to.

The effects of the pills wouldn't last forever, so I eliminated their need for sleep, eating or anything that wasn't reading. Their minds and bodies would still think that those things were necessities still, but they'd live without such luxuries for now. It was the hour for some mandatory reading.

The pair marched for hours, reading random pages and attempting in vain to keep track of them all and where they were located. My patience felt thinner than ever as they failed to complete their task. I wrote in a floor of hot coals, trying to speed up their steps. They were fast readers, but I demanded opinions now, they were on my time.

Days went by, still the books were not together. Progress had been made by both participants. I was happy with what they had managed to accomplish. They were tied in the percentage of progress that each had made. Time was up though. More drastic measures needed taken to hasten things up.

I snapped my fingers three times, then they were both taken to a secluded cave, separate still. A faux wall of rock was between the duo. There was a working door along the wall that I used to visit each reader.

Deanna was up first. She was lovingly tied to a chair with her head forced to tilt backwards. A feeding tube was ran down her throat, she was sedated but alert enough to be fed my stories. They would be digested in her abdomen and then released to her thoughts. I opened up Subjective Serendipity, then word by word, I scraped the words off each page, dutifully making sure each of the cuts were smoothly sliced onto my knife's blade.

When the book was complete, I let her rest enough to write a review on the laptop I had provided. The tube was removed, but there were a countless number of words still to go.

Corrina went next. She was also tied to a chair, but her head was forced forwards. Her glasses taken off of her face, I used eye restraints to keep her eyeballs exposed. I was controlling the bounds of reality, so I tore the first page of the same book and approached her. I was trying new tactics with both her and Deanna. Inventive methods.

"No Remorse," I whispered in her ear, then I ran the page across the surface of her eyes slowly.

The tiny gashes split open on her eyes' surfaces and they took in the words from page one.

"You'll enjoy this book," I smiled at her before slicing more of my imagination upon her corneas.

Deanna groaned disapprovingly as I made my ingress back to where she was. I was wheeling in a pole with a feeding bag, and a cart that contained a blender. She said nothing, how could she when I had dislocated her larynx, just as I did with Corrina. I would not tolerate disobedience, nor any sort of try at reckoning.

"Now that you've taken a break, time for another book," I suggested with no room for option.

I then put the next few books in the blender, then put the contents in the bag, then attached it to her feeding tube that I had reinserted as my pages were being chopped.

"Thank you for your reviews," I foreshadowed, nodding in approval as the ink reassembled my words to her mind.

Breathing was scarce with the trachea disconnected, so I knew they both had a limited time to adhere to my commands. With my stories pouring in, I dismissed myself and let the tales be told.

Corrina's eyes were red and black, full of inky blood. I saw that there was space for more slices, so I slashed little incisions and she experienced more of my brain. When her eyes were too diced to accept more cutting, I turned her skin to braille. She didn't have the knowledge of reading the ridges prior, but I had the gift to create! I untied her, but kept her will under my thumb. As her fingers traced her body, I stepped through a doorway that led to another room.

This is where I was writing the story up to that point, popping in to decide where to go next with my reviewers. Only this time, my phone was in the hands of Ali. She glared at me gleefully, undoubtedly enjoying the astonishment that I was feeling.

"I didn't write this," I growled.

"You didn't have to," Ali smirked.

"Explain."

Ali and Shannon looked at one another, then their eyes met mine.

"This girl is a fucking genius," they exclaimed collectively, moving aside so Michelle could step up.

Michelle cracked her knuckles, then she laid out how this intrusion was possible.

"Carrier pigeons, I knew to beat you, off the grid was the key. I had kept a small scrap of your special paper after the last time that I saw you, just enough to train them to hunt for it. I have raised the aviary messengers since childhood, so I knew that it was my duty to figure out where you had gone. Your own private island, you've really got a nasty God complex. Once they returned with a sliver that matched, I knew I had you. That's when my birds helped me correspond with the rest of the crew here. You never wondered why this final story was so short, like your paper supply, too caught up in your egotistical dictation to notice. I formulated a plan. Together, we tracked down everyone who had prints of your books and collected them all."

My nostrils flared at the audacity, my printed works were rare. Shelly then presented a garbage bag that contained the bindings of my written imagination. Perry took down the fake barrier that divided the room. I then saw Deanna and Corrina disappear, it was at that moment that I knew I'd never hear their full reviews, and they'd never read every sentence I had structured. What we had seen from one another, was it. They were back safely at home, healing but scarred. I wished I had left them dead from their short mentions in my technological title, but I gotten covetous for their opinions. My vanity served as my downfall.

An earthquake shook all of us, then the setting changed. We were no longer on my island, we were now in the future. A great serpent swam the cosmos, we were in the belly of this beast. 'The Pit,' was what the cult of Nephaniel called it.

Ali channeled her powers from the witchy character based on her, Clearly Alice. A back orb surrounded her left hand, while a white one orbited her right. Her eyes were opposite in which was white and which was black. She flicked her wrists towards me and Susan, encasing us in a magical dust of black and white particles.

"A hemmoraging, isn't that what you would refer to this as?"

A green transference left Susan's practically dead, limp body. I ingested the fragments of Totter infection, then my bloodstream turned to rust. I squirmed as the stream in my veins thickened to tiny metal flakes.

Shannon wasted no time in writing in a part where she was holding a machete. She hacked off all of my limbs, but I didn't bleed. I felt every cut but the rust in my hemoglobin was damming up the wounds with agonizing clots. I needed to plead with her, but she had already sawed out my jawline and had the pieces aside.

Susan began to tremble on the table, then her eye sockets went hollow, as did her gums. I already had the ending, there would be a Teether at the finish line of my story. Her eyes appeared on my face, in the same placement as described in Sphere Court, rearranging my own to match too.

Perry sat reading it as it unfolded, always the dedicated reader, she was happily invested in the printed words as my narration was pressed live by The Circadian Bulletin. She was truly an avid reader.

Shelly wrote her in a tool also, a welding device. She knew from my books that my blood would be rusted, so she soldered my amputated legs to my shoulders. As Shelly was welding, Shannon removed everything below my ribcage with long and slow strides from a saw. When they were done, my spine began to elongate, stretching and tearing itself to reach the floor. The growing pains were unbearable. My jaws were then welded to the ends of the spine, my arms welded to one of the jaw pieces each. Susan's teeth poked through my gums, spacing my own further than they were meant to. I could tell by their sensitivity that they were stripped of their enamel. The clanging and scrapes of my bellowing echoed the chamber, then my restraints began to disintegrate.

Perry looked up from the story, it was still being written in her hand, then she had her part written. She was the pogo bearer, the final part to complete my transformation. I had become my most infamous creation, a Totter Teether.

Ali was kind enough to place a lengthy mirror in front of me so that I could witness what I'd become.

Susan writhed, emitting sounds that resembled a flock of battered sheep. Her tongue wriggled in awkward vibrations, then she went silent for a minute.

"What happened to my eyes? Where are my teeth?"

Susan went into abrupt hysterics for a bit, then stopped when she heard the noises coming from me. It sounded like an ongoing car wreck as I screamed at the achiness of my teeth. They were throbbing, pinching nerves all within my gum lines. They felt rotten, but I knew they were prepped for gnawing as means of relief.

Er-nt.

I moved, cringing as my lower half creaked because of the worn out spring of the pogo stick. My legs were tired already, but this was a permanent transition.

Susan wept.

The reviewers all turned towards her, their mouths gaped when they see that she was sobbing because her spine was gone, as it had fused with my own. She had to give up herself, it was the rule of a hemmor age. Two become one, or one becomes two. It was always centered around separation and combination. Things were a little skewed now, so it played out how the girls chose it to, while keeping my ending uncontaminated.

Shannon approached cautiously, then plucked the eyelids off of our eyes. They tore away as if freshness stickers on a store product.

"Nowhere was there mention of a blinking Totter," she justified with a wicked grin.

Susan sobbed, spineless and blind. What would come of her now, well, that was up to the other Commabusters. Regarding her eyeballs, they would see our teeth gnaw for eternity. It would be almost impossible for her to die after the prolonged absorption from the DNA of a Teether. Even if she managed death, she would be reborn without the segments of her anatomy that I stole and would assemble somehow.

Our gaze fell upon the pile before me. Every book that I ever sent out was here, every tale, every misplaced comma, my life's work was nowhere where readers could ever see them.

As for who would ever read my books, the answer is the same as the question: who has ever seen a Totter?

"No one," Shelly answered for me, purposefully misspelling my pen name.

Destiny had come full circle, my restraints dissipated entirely, but my readers had disappeared. All that remained were papers all over the floor and my printed physical works. I cared about none of it, I hurt and it was time to masticate. A Network was coming, devoted followers would join me eventually and I'd have an eternity of company in The Pit. Forever gnawing, this was my *Event*. My voice reduced to the noise of mangled metal colliding, a sound that always made my teeth grind.

Also by Christopher Besonen

The Parable Collection
Midnight Parables
Parables At Dusk
Early Hour Parables
Preceeding Daybreak: Parables IV
Parable Quinate
Parable Terminus

Standalone
Troubling Stirrings In Sphere Court
Network
Subjective Serendipity

Watch for more at https://linktr.ee/BesonenHorror.

9 798869 032621